Every muscle in his body stiffened as he thought he heard a faint cry coming from the hole in the ground.

He turned on his flashlight and shone it down, seeing nothing but earth.

Had he heard her crying? Weeping because she knew this was the end of her walks? Should he go down and console her? Or let her cry in private? He had a feeling that if she was crying, she wouldn't welcome his presence.

He heard her again, only this time instead of weeping, it sounded like a scream of terror. With his gun in one hand, his flashlight in the other and adrenaline pumping through his body, he dropped down into the hole.

The first thing he saw was the penlight beam, shining at him from the floor in the distance. What he didn't see was any sign of Savannah.

"Savannah!" He yelled her name, and it echoed in the air.

He quickly walked forward, his gun leading the way and his heart pounding a million beats a minute. Where was Savannah? Why was her flashlight on the ground? What in the hell was happening?

He didn't know, but he wouldn't give up until he found her.

SCENE OF THE CRIME: THE DEPUTY'S PROOF

New York Times Bestselling Author

CARLA CASSIDY

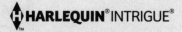

HARLEQUIN® INTRIGUE®

Recycling programs
for this product may
not exist in your area.

ISBN-13: 978-0-373-69867-7

Scene of the Crime: The Deputy's Proof

Copyright © 2015 by Carla Bracale

Printed in U.S.A.

www.Harlequin.com

Carla Cassidy is a *New York Times* bestselling author who has written more than one hundred books for Harlequin. Carla believes the only thing better than curling up with a good book to read is sitting down at the computer with a good story to write. She's looking forward to writing many more books and bringing hours of pleasure to readers.

Books by Carla Cassidy

Harlequin Intrigue

Visit the Author Profile page at
Harlequin.com for more titles.

CAST OF CHARACTERS

Savannah Sinclair—Still grieving over her older sister's murder, she has stumbled upon a secret that puts her life at risk.

Deputy Josh Griffin—A man haunted by his inability to properly investigate Shelly Sinclair's murder, and determined to protect Savannah.

Eric Baptiste—A loner who works at his mother's herb shop. Is he the man who wants to silence Savannah forever?

Mayor Jim Burns—Is his ambition so big he will kill anyone who gets in his way?

Bo McBride—The main suspect in Shelly's death. Is he afraid that Savannah knows damaging information that will point to him being a murderer?

Chad Wilson—Is he just the local grocery deliverer, or does he hide a secret obsession that will only be satisfied by Savannah's murder?

Neil Sampson—A city councilman who shares a secret with Savannah that could destroy his future political ambitions.

Chapter One

It was a perfect night for a ghost walk. The Mississippi moon was nearly hidden from view by the low-lying fog that seeped across the land and invaded the streets of the small town of Lost Lagoon.

Savannah Sinclair retied the double-beamed flashlight that hung at her waist beneath a white, gauzy, floor-length gown. She used talcum powder to lighten her face and knew that most people would think her actions were more than a little crazy.

Maybe she'd been a little crazy for the past two years, since the night her older sister, her best friend, Shelly, had been murdered and found floating in the lagoon.

From that night forward, Savannah's life had been forever changed. *She* had been forever changed, and what she planned to do at midnight tonight just proved that Shelly's death still haunted her in a profound way she couldn't get past.

She stared at her ghostly countenance in the bathroom mirror and wondered, if Shelly's murder had been solved and her killer arrested, would things be different?

She whirled away from the mirror and left the bathroom. The clock on the nightstand in the bedroom indicated that it was eleven thirty. Time to move.

She turned off all the lights in the four-bedroom house that had once been home to her family, grabbed a palm-sized penlight and then slipped out the back door.

The dark night closed in around her, and she glanced at her nearest neighbor's house, satisfied that all the lights were off and her neighbor, Jeffrey Allen, was surely in bed. She used the penlight in her hand to guide her toward a large bush at the back of the yard.

Shoving several of the leafy branches aside, she revealed a hole big enough for a person to drop into. She knew there were earthen steps to aid in the three-foot drop, and she easily accomplished it, finding herself at the beginning of a narrow earthen tunnel.

She'd discovered the tunnel last summer when she'd been working in the yard. Initially she had to crouch for several feet before the tunnel descended deep enough that she could stand in an upright position and walk.

Half the town already thought she was crazy, gone around the bend because of her parents' abandonment, her brother's rages and the murder of her sister.

If they only knew what she did on moonless nights when she wasn't working the night shift at the Pirate's Inn, they'd probably have her locked up in an insane asylum for the rest of her life. But there was a rhyme and reason to her madness.

The tunnel system was like a spider web running under the town, although Savannah had only explored one corridor, the one that would take her directly to the place where her sister had been murdered.

She moved confidently with the aid of the bright but tiny beam of her penlight leading the way. It had been rumored that Lost Lagoon had once been home to a band of pirates, and she suspected these tunnels had been made by them years and years ago.

She occasionally moved by dark passageways she had never explored and wondered if anyone had been in them in the last hundred years or so.

She hadn't told anyone of her discovery of the tunnels. They were her secret, her voyage to the last link to her sister. It took her a little over fifteen minutes to reach her destination, a set of six old wooden planks embedded into the ground that led up to another hole beneath a bush at the base of a cypress tree.

She shut off her penlight, climbed up the planks and crouched behind the tree trunk. At this time on a Friday night, most of the town would be at Jimmy's Place, a popular bar and grill on Main Street.

But moonless Friday nights when the fog rolled in— the teenagers in town knew those were the nights that Shelly's ghost walked the night.

Savannah could hear them, a small group of teenage girls giggling behind a row of bushes that separated the swampy lagoon from the edge of town. Set in the center of the row of bushes was a stone bench where her sister and her boyfriend, Bo McBride, used to sit at night and talk about their future, but Shelly had never gotten a future.

Between the bushes and the swamp was just enough solid ground for a "ghost" to walk in front of the bushes and the bench and disappear into the wooded, swampy area on the other side.

She remained hidden for several minutes until she thought it was just about midnight, and then she turned on the flashlight strapped around her waist beneath the gauzy white gown. The double-sided beam produced an otherworldly glow from her head to her toes.

Performance time, she thought. Her role as Shelly's ghost required very little of her, an appropriate costume but no script to memorize. She started to walk across the "stage." She walked slowly, her head half-turned away and her long dark hair hiding her features from her audience.

"There she is!" A young female voice squealed.

"It's Shelly. It's really Shelly," another voice cried out.

Savannah embraced the sound of her sister's name into her heart as she continued her walk. Tears burned in her eyes, but she swallowed against them. Shelly's ghost didn't cry. She just walked across the place where she'd been murdered and then disappeared almost as quickly as she'd appeared.

To the continuing squeals of her sister's name, Savannah reached the woods on the other side of the "stage." She shut off the flashlight at her waist and headed for a tangled growth of vines behind which was the small entrance of a cave. The opening of the cave was hidden and couldn't be seen unless you knew what you were looking for.

She quickly moved the concealing vines aside and clicked on her little penlight, using it after she'd entered the fairly large cave that led downhill. The cave narrowed somewhat as it continued but remained wide enough that a pirate could push trunks of treasure or buckets of jewels through it.

This passageway eventually intersected with the one that would take her to her backyard, a perfect escape route for the ghost of the dead.

She moved quickly, eager now to get back to the house where she lived. It was the house she'd grown up in, but it hadn't felt like home since two months after Shelly's murder, when her parents had left town and moved to a small retirement community in Florida.

They'd left the house for Savannah and her older brother, Mac, to live in. Mac had married and moved out months before, leaving Savannah in the house that contained far too many haunting memories.

She felt a cathartic relief and a little bit of guilt as she reached the earthen steps that would bring her up into her backyard.

Everyone in Lost Lagoon loved a good ghost story, she told herself. The town was steeped in stories of the walking dead. The ghosts of dead pirates were rumored to walk the hallways of Pirate's Inn.

Savannah had been working there as night manager for a little over a year, and while she occasionally heard odd bumps and thumps in the night, she'd never seen a ghost.

But the rumors of sightings of apparitions were repeated again and again by thrilled townspeople and occasional tourists. The ghost of an old, toothless hag supposedly appeared in the alley beside the Lost Lagoon Cafe, and several people had sworn they'd seen the faint wisp of ghostly figures around Mama Baptiste's Apothecary Shop.

She turned off her penlight, stepped up out of the tunnel and squeaked in surprise as she saw a tall, dark figure standing before her. She fumbled to turn on her penlight once again and found herself face-to-face with Deputy Josh Griffin.

"Hi, Savannah. Busy night?" he asked.

Her heart sank as she realized she'd been busted.

JOSH SHONE HIS own flashlight on the slender, dark-haired woman. Her doe-like brown eyes were huge in a face that was unnaturally pale. Her lower lip trembled even as she raised her chin and glared at him defiantly.

"If you're going to arrest me, then just get on with it," she exclaimed.

"How about we get out of the dark and go inside and talk about my options," he replied.

Savannah Sinclair and the murder of her sister, Shelly, had haunted Josh for a long time. Before the murder Savannah had been a lively, charming twenty-seven-year-old who was often seen out and about town.

"Okay," she replied. Despite her initial upthrust

of her chin, as he walked just behind her he saw her shoulders slump forward and felt the energy that had momentarily radiated from her disappear.

Despite the ridiculous outfit she wore, he noticed the slight sway of her slender hips beneath the gauzy material, could smell the faint scent of a fresh floral perfume that emanated from her.

The few times he'd seen her since her sister's murder, he'd been filled with guilt. The consensus at the time had been that Shelly had been murdered by her then-boyfriend, Bo McBride, and that law enforcement simply hadn't found the evidence to make an arrest. Josh knew how little had actually been done in the investigation.

But that was then and this was now, and it had taken him weeks to figure out the mystery of "Shelly's ghost." He now had questions for Savannah that he wanted answered.

She opened the back door that led into the kitchen. She turned on the overhead light and gestured him toward a chair at the round wooden table.

"If you don't mind, I'd like to change clothes before you decide to take me in," she said. She didn't give him a chance to reply but instead left the room.

Josh sat in a chair at the table and looked around. Red roosters danced across the bottoms of beige curtains at the window, and a hen and rooster salt and pepper shaker set perched on the pristine stove top. Other than a coffeemaker, the countertops were bare.

There was an emptiness, a void of life in the room,

as if it were a designer home where nobody really lived. He heard water running in another room, and a few minutes later, Savannah returned.

She'd changed out of the gauzy gown and into a pair of jeans that hugged her long slender legs and a blue-and-gold T-shirt advertising the Pirate's Inn. She sat across from him at the table. She'd obviously washed her face, for her color was more natural. Her cheeks were faintly pink.

"So, are you going to arrest me?" she asked. Gone was the defiance, leaving behind only a weary resignation in her voice.

"What would I arrest you for? Impersonating a ghost?" he asked with a touch of amusement. "I don't want to arrest you, Savannah. I want to talk to you. What are you doing? Why are you pretending to be Shelly's ghost?"

Her long-lashed brown eyes gazed at him, and she tucked a strand of the long, silky-looking dark hair behind one ear. "How did you know that I'd appear out of the bush in my backyard?"

"I've been tracking the sightings of Shelly's ghost for about a month," he replied. "I saw your performance a couple of weeks ago and instantly realized it was you, but I couldn't figure out how you appeared and disappeared and got back here without anyone seeing you. So, I've been staking out your house and watching your movements."

Her face paled slightly. "You've been stalking me?"

"Basically, yeah," he admitted. "But I have to say, you aren't an exciting person to stalk."

Her cheeks grew pink again. "Sorry if I bored you with my life. Aren't there other people you should be stalking? Don't you have any real crime fighting to do?"

"Things have been pretty quiet since we managed to get Roger Cantor arrested," he replied. The affable coach of the high school had been exposed as a deadly stalker and was now behind bars. "And you didn't answer my question. What are you doing pretending to be Shelly's ghost?"

"Entertaining the locals," she replied airily, but her dark eyes simmered with a depth of emotion that belied her words. "And you didn't answer mine. How exactly did you figure out that I'd appear by the bush in the backyard after one of my ghostly walks?"

"The last time you pulled your stunt, I was here, watching the backyard to see if you'd sneak across the lawn. To my surprise, you came up from under the ground."

Josh had always been attracted to Savannah's high spirits, her beauty and more than a touch of sexy flirtation that had always lit her eyes when they happened to encounter each other. But that had been before her sister's murder, and the woman who sat across from him now appeared achingly fragile, a mere shell of what she'd once been.

A touch of guilt swept through him again. As a lawman, his job was to solve crimes and get the guilty behind bars. But officially Shelly's case remained an open one, without resolution.

"There's a tunnel," she finally said. Her finger traced

an indecipherable pattern on the top of the wooden table, and her gaze followed her finger's movements.

"A tunnel?" Josh felt like he was attempting to pull a confession from a hardened criminal.

She stopped the movement of her hand and looked at him once again. "There's a tunnel that runs from the backyard to a tree near the lagoon where Shelly was murdered. I discovered it about a year ago."

"What would a tunnel be doing in your backyard?" he asked.

Her slender shoulders moved up and down in a shrug. "I guess you'd have to ask the person who dug it, but it looks like it was made a long, long time ago. Maybe it was used to transport goods from the lagoon to here by the pirates who once lived around here."

Josh frowned thoughtfully. Lost Lagoon had a history rich in pirate lore. He supposed it was possible that pirates could have unloaded their treasures onto little boats to navigate the small lagoon and then bring them here, where they might have had an inland camp.

He focused his attention back on her. "You haven't answered my question. Why, Savannah? Why are you doing this?"

He studied her intently, wanting her to explain, to tell him what the payoff was for pretending to be her sister's ghost. She frowned and looked out the darkened window.

Josh was a patient man. It was one of his strengths as a deputy. He leaned back in his chair, not willing to go anywhere until he had the answer he needed from her.

Was she crazy, as many people thought? Had the murder of her sister, the destruction of her family and her own isolation from everything and everyone caused mental illness of some sort?

She finally looked back at him and leaned forward. Her hair came untucked from the back of her ear, the long dark strands shining beneath the hanging light over the table.

"A month after Shelly's murder, my parents forbade us ever to speak her name again," she began. Her dark gaze went over his shoulder to the bare wall behind him. "They packed all of her things away in the storage shed out back and pretended she had never existed."

She looked back at him, her eyes filled with a depth of simmering emotion. "I wasn't ready to say goodbye to my sister, my best friend and the person I'd shared a bedroom with since I was born. As time passed and Bo left town, everyone stopped talking about Shelly. It was as if she had never existed anywhere at any time. Even after my parents left town and I tried to talk to Mac about Shelly, he shut me down. He was so angry, still is so angry. He definitely didn't want to hear Shelly's name or anything I had to say about her."

Josh understood her pain. He'd lost a twin brother when he'd been fifteen years old, and he knew for the rest of his life he'd feel as if an integral piece of himself was missing.

"I found the tunnel a year ago," Savannah continued. "It took me weeks to get up the nerve to go down inside and explore where it went. When I finally did and realized it came up next to the place where Shelly had been murdered, I came up with the ghost plan."

"But why? What do you get out of pretending to be her ghost?"

"I get to hear squealing teenagers say her name. I make sure nobody forgets about her. I keep her alive by pretending to be her apparition in death." She shook her head. "I know it sounds crazy and you probably can't understand it, but for those few moments when people are crying out Shelly's name, I feel better. I feel as if she's still with me."

"It's dangerous," Josh replied. "You're sneaking out of your house alone in the middle of the night to go down into a tunnel that you don't even know is safe. There could be a cave-in, or somebody could come after you while you're doing your little show."

A whisper of a smile curved her lips, and for a moment Josh saw the semblance of the young woman she'd once been. "Actually, a couple of weeks ago Bo McBride did come after me. Apparently his new girlfriend, Claire Silver, told him about Shelly's ghost and encouraged him to see the spectacle. I'd just finished my walk when he jumped over the bushes and chased me into the woods. I jumped into my rabbit hole and disappeared."

"But that's my point," Josh protested. "You disappear down that tunnel, and if anything happened to you, nobody would know you were in trouble." He leaned forward. "I want to check out this tunnel."

Her eyes widened, and her gaze slid away from his.

"I don't think that's necessary. I've been using it for almost a year, and it's perfectly safe."

"I'd still like to check it out for myself," he countered. She looked at him again, and he knew in his gut that she was hiding something. "I figure you've got two choices."

"And I figure I'm not going to like either one of them," she retorted.

"You can take me down through that tunnel and I can see for myself that it's safe and secure, or I can get a backhoe in here to fill in the entrance in your backyard."

She sat up straighter in her chair, a flash of anger in her eyes. "You can't do that. My backyard is private property."

"I can do it," he replied calmly. "That hole is a danger. A small child could fall down it. I can make a case to have it filled in without your permission for the safety of the community."

She glared at him. It was the most emotion he'd seen from her since her sister's death. "Fine, I'll take you down into the tunnel."

Josh nodded and stood. "Why don't we plan on around noon tomorrow? I'll come here and we can check it out."

She stood as well, her body vibrating with tension. "Don't take this away from me, Josh. It's all I have in my life."

He had a ridiculous impulse to step forward and pull her into his arms. Instead he stepped toward the back door. "I'm just trying to keep you safe, Savannah. That's my job."

"If I felt unsafe, I would have called Sheriff Walker," she replied.

"Maybe you aren't in a mental state to know what's safe and what isn't."

He knew he'd spoken the wrong words by the flash of unbridled annoyance that filled her eyes and stiffened her stance.

"Contrary to popular belief, I'm perfectly sane. I know people think I've become a weird recluse who only comes out at night to work at the local haunted hotel, but that's my choice. The way I live my life is nobody's business but my own."

"Point taken," Josh replied. He opened the back door. "I'll see you at noon tomorrow. Good night, Savannah."

She shut the door behind him with more force than was necessary, and he headed for his patrol car parked at the curb in front of her house.

He got into the car and started the engine but didn't immediately drive away. Instead he sat and stared at her house. No lights shone from the front windows just as very little light had shone from her eyes on the occasional times he'd seen her in the last two years.

Despite his intense attraction to her two years ago, since that time he'd tried not to think about her. It was only curiosity about Shelly's "ghost" that had brought him here tonight.

Guilt was a terrible thing, he thought as he finally pulled away from the curb. Savannah was broken.

She'd been broken since Shelly's murder…a murder that had never been investigated as vigorously as it should have been.

As a deputy, Josh had followed orders, but as a decent man, he had known nobody was doing enough to close the case. Closure might have made a difference to Savannah.

Yes, she was broken, but he had no hero complex. He wasn't the man to fix her, but what he could do was make sure she was safe if she insisted on doing her ghostly walks.

He couldn't go back in time and do things differently in the case of her sister, but he could see to it that if Savannah insisted on continuing her haunting ghostly walks, at least the tunnel she used was safe.

Chapter Two

Savannah awoke with the unaccustomed emotion of anger tightening her chest. It had been so long since she hadn't awakened with the familiar grief that it took her a moment to recognize the new feeling that pressed so tight inside her.

Then she remembered the night before and Deputy Josh Griffin and knew immediately he was the source of her unusual anger. He was going to be here at noon and insist he go down into the tunnel with her, and when he did, he'd ruin everything.

He'd see that it wasn't just a single tunnel but rather a network of tunnels. Word would get out, people would start to explore and her nights of ghost walking would be over forever. She'd never hear Shelly's name again except in the deepest recesses of her broken heart.

She rolled over in bed and stared at the opposite side of the bedroom. The wall was covered with pictures of Shelly and Savannah, hugging each other when they were ten and eleven, Shelly dressed for prom at sixteen with Savannah posing with her, moments captured in time of the closeness of the two.

A desk held items that had been special to Shelly—the dried flower corsage that Bo McBride had given to her on prom night, a framed picture of the Manhattan skyline at twilight, a ceramic frog and a variety of other knickknacks.

Savannah had unpacked the items from the shed after Mac had moved out, comforted by the little pieces of Shelly that now remained in the room the two had shared for so many years of their lives.

She glanced at the clock on the nightstand. Just after ten. Normally she'd sleep until at least noon or one due to her overnight work hours at the Pirate's Inn. She'd be sucking wind tonight if she didn't get a nap in sometime during the afternoon or early evening.

Minutes later, as she stood beneath the shower spray, her thoughts turned to Josh Griffin. Before Shelly's death, she'd thought him one of the most handsome, hot single men in town.

He'd only grown more handsome in the past two years. As he'd sat at the table the night before, she couldn't help but notice on some level how his dark hair enhanced the crystal blue of his eyes.

It had been impossible not to notice how his broad shoulders had filled out his khaki deputy shirt and that he'd smelled of spicy cologne that had stirred her senses on some primal level.

She didn't want to like Josh Griffin. As far as she

was concerned, he was just part of the law enforcement in town that had botched her sister's murder case. And now he was going to ruin the only thing that made her feel just a little bit alive.

She dressed in a pair of denim shorts and a light blue T-shirt and then made a pot of coffee. The silence of the house was comfortable to her. When she and Mac had shared the house, there had always been shouting and cursing. Now the silence was like an old familiar friend.

Mac had been one of the loudest voices proclaiming the guilt of Bo McBride in Shelly's murder. But he'd always thought Bo wasn't good enough for her. Sometimes Savannah wondered about her brother...but she never allowed the perverse thought to take hold.

She sat at the table to drink her coffee and stared out the window that gave her not only a view of her own backyard but also a partial view of her neighbor's.

Jeffrey Allen was out there now, weeding a flower bed, his bald head covered against the July sun by a large straw hat. Jeffrey wasn't a pleasant man. In his midfifties, he worked as a mechanic at the local car repair shop and for the past five years or so had had a contentious relationship with the Sinclair family.

She only hoped he finished his lawn work before Josh arrived to check out the tunnel. The last thing she wanted to do was give Jeffrey any ammunition to work with to get her out of this house.

He'd made it clear that he wanted to buy her house

for some of his family members to move into, but Savannah had no plans ever to sell.

By eleven forty-five, Jeffrey had disappeared from his yard and gone back into his house, and a nervous energy flooded through Savannah's veins. Within a few minutes, Josh would arrive and destroy the one thing that had kept Shelly relevant beyond her death.

Savannah was still seated at the kitchen table when Josh appeared at the back door. She wanted to pretend he wasn't there, ignore the soft knock he delivered, but she knew he wasn't going to just go away, especially since he could see her through the window.

Reluctantly she got up to let him inside. Josh worked the night shift, like Savannah, and so instead of his uniform, he was clad in a pair of jeans and a black T-shirt.

With his slightly unruly black hair and his usual sexy grin curving sensual lips, he looked like the proverbial irresistible bad boy. He was a bad boy. He was about to rock her world in a very adverse way.

"Good afternoon," he said when she opened the door.

"Not particularly," she replied, embracing the alien emotion of the anger she'd awakened with. It felt so fresh, so different from the pervasive grief that had possessed her for so long. "It would be a good day if you'd kept your nose out of my business."

He frowned, the expression doing nothing to distract from his handsome, chiseled features. "Savannah, I'm not the enemy here."

Yes, he was. He just didn't realize it yet. Right now

he was the beginning of the end of her world. With even Shelly's ghost gone, Savannah didn't know who she was or where she belonged.

"Let's just get this over with," she replied. She noticed that he carried a high-beam flashlight, and she walked to the cabinet under the kitchen sink and grabbed a flashlight for herself.

As she followed Josh out the back door, she hoped his shoulders got stuck in the hole, then realized he would probably somehow manage to get out anyway and bring in that backhoe he'd talked about the night before.

She just had to come to terms with the fact that he was about to discover not just her secret, but a secret that had been hidden from the entire town for who knew how long.

As they reached the bush, she stepped in front of him and caught a scent of the sexy cologne she'd noticed the night before. It only aggravated her more. "I'll go first," she said and bent down to shove aside the branches to reveal the hole.

She used the narrow earthen steps to go down. "Okay, your turn," she said and moved away so that he could drop in.

He didn't use the steps but landed gracefully on the ground. Apparently a three-foot drop wasn't a big deal for a tall man with long legs.

He clicked on his flashlight and shone it straight ahead. "Wow, who would have thought?" he exclaimed in shock.

From this vantage point, the other passageway entrances weren't visible. "See, it's safe as can be," she said. "The earth is hard-packed and solid."

He shone his light beyond her. "I want you to take me to where you come up to do your nightly walks by the swamp."

This was what she'd been hoping to avoid, but she knew there was no way to stop him. "Follow me," she said in resignation. It would take only about three minutes for him to know that "her" tunnel wasn't the only one down here.

"Did it ever occur to you that the person who murdered Shelly might have used this tunnel to escape the scene of the crime?" he asked after only a step or two.

"You mean the murderer you all never caught?" The anger was back. She stopped and turned to face him, her light shining in his eyes.

He winced. "You don't believe that Bo McBride was responsible?"

"No, even though nearly everyone else in town, including all of you lawmen, believed him guilty. I never believed in my heart that he'd hurt Shelly. He loved her more than he loved himself."

"Did you know he's back in town to stay?" Josh asked. "And turn that light away," he added with an edge of irritation.

She lowered the beam to the center of his chest. "He's been back for over a month. I know he's living with Claire Silver because the creepy stalker that was after her burned Bo's family house down. I also know he and Claire are trying to find the truth about who murdered Shelly. When he chased me that night, I already suspected he was back in Lost Lagoon to stay."

"Look, I'm not down in this dungeon to reinvestigate your sister's murder. I'm sorry how things turned out and that nobody was ever arrested, but that's not why we're down here."

"You were the one who brought it up," she replied.

Suddenly she just wanted to get this over with, get back into her silent house where she lived with just memories of the family who had once filled the quiet with life.

She turned around and continued walking, and when she came to the first passageway that shot off the main tunnel, she heard Josh gasp in surprise.

"I thought you said this was just one tunnel, from your backyard directly to the edge of the swamp." He shone his light down the new tunnel.

Once again she turned to face him. "I lied. There are tons of tunnels down here. I think they run under the entire town, and now that you know that, everything is going to be ruined for me. You'll feel obligated to tell somebody, and word will get out, and there will be tons of people down here exploring everywhere."

To her horror, she burst into tears…the first tears she had shed since the day they had buried her sister.

JOSH WASN'T SURE what shocked him more, the discovery of the other tunnels or Savannah's unexpected tears. No, they weren't just simple tears. She leaned against the earthen wall and sobbed as if her heart was breaking.

"Savannah," he said softly, and he touched her arm. She jerked away and cried harder. "Savannah, please don't cry." Not knowing what to do, unaccustomed to sobbing females, he tucked his flashlight into the back of the waist of his pants and pulled her into his arms.

She stiffened against him and then melted into him, crying into the hollow of his throat. Although she was tall, she felt small and fragile in his arms. Her hair smelled of wildflowers, and she fit neatly against him.

It lasted only a couple of heartbeats, and then she twirled out of his embrace and swiped at her tears as if angry at herself for the display of emotion. "I'm sorry. I didn't mean for that to happen."

She faced him, the eerie illumination of their flashlights casting dancing shadows on her features. "You just have no idea what you're taking away from me."

"Why don't we continue on, and we can talk about it all when we're above ground again," he suggested and pulled his flashlight out of his waistband.

She nodded and turned to lead the way once again. Josh tried to keep pace with her, but he slowed each time he passed yet another tunnel that branched off the one they followed. And there were plenty of branches.

Throughout the walk, he could tell they were descending, although it was impossible to tell just how deep they were beneath the ground.

He counted at least seven branches of darkened tunnels by the time they reached the end of the main one.

Plank steps led upward. They hadn't spoken a word to each other as they'd travelled forward.

He'd been too amazed by the subterranean world he'd been introduced to by Savannah. Where did the other tunnels lead? How big was the network? Who knew about it besides Savannah?

He was fairly sure the answer to the question was that nobody except Savannah and now him knew about the underground network. Otherwise he would have heard about it before now. Lost Lagoon was a small town, and a secret this big would have been revealed.

He followed her up the plank steps that led them next to a large cypress tree surrounded by thick brush. The ground was spongy beneath his feet, although not wet enough to cover his shoes. There was nobody in the area, and he was glad that nobody was around to see them ascend from the ground.

Directly in front of them was the swath of land where Shelly's "ghost" walked. He looked at Savannah, whose features were void of emotion. "So, you walk across here and then what? How do you get back to this same entrance to get back home?"

"I don't. On the other side of the path is a hidden cave that leads back to the tunnel we were just in." She didn't wait for his response but quickly walked across the path that was her "stage" on nights she performed her ghost routine.

Josh hurried after her, his mind still reeling from where he'd been and what he'd seen. When they reached the other side, he followed her up a small hill through thick woods.

She stopped and pulled a tangle of vines and brush aside to reveal the mouth of a cave. Once again a sense of shock swept through him.

He'd been a deputy in Lost Lagoon for the past ten years. He'd moved to the small town from Georgia when he was twenty-one to take the position of deputy. Ten years and he hadn't heard a whisper of the presence of the underground network.

He followed her into the mouth of the cave and found himself again in a tunnel that merged into the one they'd used from Savannah's backyard.

They were silent as they returned the way they had come. The initial excitement and surprise of what he'd seen had passed. Instead he was acutely attuned to the air of defeat that emanated from Savannah while she walked slowly in front of him.

He dreaded the conversation to come. There was no way he could keep this information to himself. Who knew what might be found in the other tunnels? Who knew where they led? It was a historical find that should be made public to the appropriate authorities.

What surprised him was that Savannah had possessed the nerve to go down there and explore on her own. It must have been frightening the first time she'd decided to drop down that hole and follow the tunnel.

When they came back up in her backyard, the July sun and humidity were relentless. He hadn't realized how much cooler the tunnels had been until now.

"Come on inside and I'll get us something cold to drink," she said without enthusiasm.

It wasn't the best invitation he'd ever gotten from a woman, but he was hot and thirsty, and they weren't finished with their business yet.

Once inside, he sat in the same chair at the table where he'd sat the night before. She went to the cabinet and pulled down two glasses.

She turned to look at him, her eyes dull and lifeless. "Sweet tea okay?"

"Anything cold is fine," he replied.

She opened the refrigerator and poured the tea. She then carried the glasses to the table and sat across from him. Her eyes were now dark pools of aching sadness, so aching that he couldn't stand to look at them.

He took a sip of the cold tea and then stared down into the glass. "You know I can't keep this a secret," he finally said.

"I know you can't keep it a secret forever," she replied.

He gazed at her, and this time in her eyes he saw a tiny spark of life, of hope. He steeled himself for the argument he had a feeling was about to happen.

God, it just took that single spark in her eyes for him to remember the woman she'd been, and he couldn't help the swift curl of heat that warmed his belly. It was a heat of the visceral attraction he'd forgotten had once existed where she was concerned.

"Give me one more night," she said. "Just let me have one more walk before you tell anyone about the tunnels." She leaned forward, her eyes now positively glowing with focus. "One final walk, Josh. At least let me have that before it all blows up."

"Savannah…"

"Those tunnels have been a secret for who knows how long," she said, interrupting him. "Can't you just keep them a secret for another week or so?"

He told himself it was too big, that he should report on what he'd found out immediately. He sat up straighter in his chair, determined to do the right thing, and then she surprised him. She reached across the table and covered one of his hands with hers.

"Please, Josh, all I'm asking for is a week. I can do a final ghost walk next Friday night, and then you can tell whoever you want about the tunnels."

Her hand was warm, almost fevered over his, and for just a moment, as he stared into the dark pools of her eyes, he forgot what they'd been talking about.

He mentally shook himself and pulled his hand from beneath hers. Duty battled with the desire to do something for her, something to make up for letting her down two years before when he should have chosen real justice over his job.

He took another drink of tea and then stood. He needed to think, and at the moment he was finding it difficult to think rationally.

"I assume you're working your usual shift tonight at the inn?" He moved toward the back door. He needed to get away from her winsome eyes, the floral scent of her that filled his head.

"Eleven to seven," she replied. "Why?"

"I need to think about everything. I won't say anything to anyone today, and I'll stop by the Pirate's Inn tonight sometime during my shift and let you know what I've decided to do."

She opened her mouth as if to make one more plea, but closed it and nodded. "Then I guess I'll see you sometime tonight."

He left her house and walked around to his car. No patrol car today, just a nice red convertible sports car that most women would definitely consider a boy toy.

He'd bought the car a year ago, and the day he signed the ownership papers, his head had been filled with the memory of his twin brother, Jacob.

When the two boys had been growing up, they'd dreamed of owning a car like this…flashy and fast and nothing like the old family car their parents had driven. That old car had been held together by string and hope because new cars cost money the Griffin family didn't have.

Driving to his house, he once again thought about the surprising discovery of the tunnels. The presence of them had been such a shock. Had they been made by pirates who were rumored to have used the Lost Lagoon town as a base camp? Would there be treasures and artifacts in one of those passageways that would identify who had made them and why?

It was much easier to think about the tunnels than about the woman he'd just left. But thoughts of Savannah intruded. Of the two sisters, he'd always thought she was the prettiest. She was softer, a little bit shyer than Shelly, but she'd drawn Josh to her.

She'd had a smile that lit up her face and made it impossible not to smile back at her. He wondered if she had smiled at all in the last two years.

He pulled into the driveway of his three-bedroom ranch house. He'd bought the house when it was just a shell and had added amenities like an extra-long whirlpool tub for a tall man to relax in and a walkout door from the bedroom to a private patio. He'd also put in all the bells and whistles in the kitchen area. He'd been told by the builder that it would be good for resale value.

The cost of living in Lost Lagoon was relatively low, and his salary was good, as few lawmen would choose to spend their careers in a small swamp town.

When he got inside, he sat at his kitchen table with a bottle of cold beer, and once again his head filled with visions of Savannah.

One week. That was all she'd asked for. Just seven days. But was it even right for him to indulge her in one more ghost walk? Wasn't it better just to end it all now and hope that she got some sort of help for the grief that had obviously held her in its grip for far too long?

And what if Sheriff Trey Walker found out that he'd known about the tunnels and hadn't come forward immediately? Trey was a tough guy who demanded

100 percent loyalty from his men. Would Josh be putting his job on the line to give Savannah what she'd asked for?

He took a long sip of his beer and reviewed his options—none of which he liked.

Chapter Three

Savannah stood behind the reception desk in the large quiet lobby of the Pirate's Inn. The inn had two stories, and the centerpiece of the lobby was a huge, tacky treasure chest that the inn's owner, Donnie Albright, had been repainting for the last couple of weeks.

He'd finished the six-foot-tall chest itself, painting it a bright gold, but he still had to spruce up the oversized papier-mâché and Styrofoam jewels and strings of pearls that filled the chest.

He was also in the process of re-carpeting the guest rooms, all in anticipation of the amusement park that had bought land and was building on a ridge above the small city.

Most of the businesses were eager for the park to be done, knowing that it would bring in tourists who would shop and spend their money in town. There were plenty of people in town who wanted Lost Lagoon to be "found" and hoped that would happen with the large amusement park under construction nearby.

At the moment, the last thing on Savannah's mind

was the new pirate-themed park. It was a little after 2:00 a.m., and Josh hadn't come in yet to tell her his decision about giving her one final walk before telling other people about the tunnels.

She sat in a raised chair and began to doodle on a notepad. There was only one couple staying in the inn tonight. Beth and Greg Hemming stayed in a room at the inn once a month. They had four children, all under the age of six, and Savannah suspected the night out was not so much about romance, but more about a good night of uninterrupted sleep.

For years the inn had mostly catered to occasional people who came to Lost Lagoon to visit with family members. It was rare that real tourists stopped in for a room for the night unless they were lost and desperate to spend the night someplace before returning to their journey.

Shelly had worked as the night manager before her murder. Savannah had taken on the same job a year ago. She was certain it was the most boring job in town.

She had a degree from a culinary school and had at one time entertained the idea of opening a restaurant in town. Lost Lagoon had a pizza place, George's Diner, which was just a cheap hamburger joint, and the café. There was no place for anyone in town to have a real fine dining experience.

That was why she had been living at home, working at the café and saving her money before Shelly's murder. But the loss of her sister had also stolen Savannah's dreams.

A rap on the front door drew her attention, and she grabbed the ring of keys that would unlock the front door. The inn was always locked up for security purposes when she arrived for her shift at eleven.

She rounded the monstrous, gaudy treasure chest to see Josh standing outside. Her heart fluttered unexpectedly at the sight of him, so tall and handsome in his khaki uniform.

It was impossible to tell what news he brought by the lack of expression on his face. She fumbled with the key and finally got the door unlocked to allow him inside.

"Busy night?" she asked as she led him back to the reception area where, in front of the desk, two sofas faced each other and were separated by a large square wooden coffee table.

"Probably no busier than yours," he replied. He sat on one end of a sofa, and she sat on the other. "Any guests in the house?"

"Beth and Greg Hemming are in room 202."

"No sightings of old Peg Leg or his drunken friend?" There was a touch of amusement in his eyes as he mentioned the most popular "ghosts" in town.

"Donnie probably made up that story about pirate ghosts haunting the hallways when he first bought this place years ago," she replied and wished he'd just get to the point.

"With the new pirate theme park going up, I imagine Donnie is anticipating lots of guests in the future."

"There are certainly going to be big changes around

here when the park is finished next summer," she replied.

"Whoever thought Lost Lagoon, Mississippi, would become a family vacation destination? I expect we'll see some new businesses popping up in the near future."

"Josh," she said impatiently.

"Okay, you don't want small talk. You want to know what I've decided to do about the tunnels." The blue of his eyes darkened slightly.

She had a sinking feeling in the pit of her stomach. If eyes were the windows to the soul, then she was about to be bitterly disappointed.

"I stewed about it all day. You know I have to tell, but I'm willing to wait until next Saturday on one condition. Friday night, when you do your final walk, I go with you."

"I've been making these walks alone for the last year. It isn't necessary for you to come with me," she protested. He threatened her just a little bit. He was too sexy, his smile was too warm. He radiated a vibrant energy that felt dangerous to her.

"That's the deal, Savannah. I go with you next Friday night, or tomorrow I tell Trey about the tunnels."

She could tell by his firm tone that he meant it. She should be grateful that he had given her as much as he had. "All right," she said. "I appreciate you giving me one last walk. I go down into the tunnel about eleven thirty or so. If you aren't by the bush at that time next Friday, I won't wait for you."

"Don't worry. I'll be there," he assured her and stood.

She got up as well and followed him back to the door. "So, we have a date next Friday night," he said, the charming amusement back in his eyes.

"A date under duress," she replied coyly.

He pushed open the door to leave but turned back to look at her. "You know, you might try walking in the sunshine sometime. It's so much better than walking in the shadows."

He didn't wait for a reply but turned and walked away. She locked the door after him and returned to the chair behind the desk.

She didn't even want to contemplate his parting words. He knew nothing about her, nothing about her life…her loss. All she had to do was see him one last time, next Friday night, and then she wouldn't have to see Deputy Josh Griffin again.

The night passed uneventfully, and by seven, when owner Donnie Albright showed up to relieve her, she was exhausted. She'd spent most of the quiet night as she usually did, sitting and trying not to think, not to feel.

Once at home, she changed out of the tailored blouse and black slacks she wore to work and into a sleeveless cotton nightgown and then fell into bed. The dark shades at her bedroom window kept out the sunlight, and she didn't have to worry about phone calls or unexpected guests interrupting her sleep.

Since Mac had moved out, the only person who ever came by the house was Chad Wilson, who delivered groceries to her once a week on Thursday afternoons.

Because she was off Thursdays and Fridays, she always got special items to cook on those days, meals she might have served customers in her own restaurant if her world hadn't fallen apart.

She finally fell asleep and dreamed of days gone by, when Shelly and Bo were a couple and she often spent time with them. Bo often teased that he was the luckiest guy in the world, with two beautiful women on his arms. He'd been like a brother to her, and she'd grieved the loss of his friendship almost as deeply as she did Shelly.

Her dream transformed, and a vision of Josh filled her mind. He held her in his arms, his body fitting close against her own as his lips covered hers in a kiss that seared fire through her.

She awakened irritated that the sexy lawman had held any place at all in her dreams.

For the next four days, she went to work each night and came home each morning and slept. In the late afternoons, when she was awake, she vegged out in front of the television, trying not to think about the fact that Friday night would be her final tribute to her sister.

She was almost grateful on Thursday afternoon when Chad showed up with the bags of groceries she'd ordered the day before from the grocery store.

Although she'd always found the thirtysomething deliveryman a bit odd, he brought her not only the things she wanted to cook but also a wealth of gossip.

If Josh hadn't held up his end of their bargain, she would know about it from Chad. He'd tell her all about the discovery of the tunnels and the exploration that was taking place.

She answered his knock on the back door and allowed him and his grocery bags inside the kitchen. "How are you doing today, Savannah?" he asked with his usual good cheer. As always, his dark brown hair stood up in spikes, and his caramel-colored eyes danced around the room as if unable to focus on any one spot.

"Good. How about you?" she asked. He placed the bags on the table, and she began to unload them.

"I've been busy today. Old Ethel Rogers fell and broke her hip last week, so I made a delivery to her earlier. You look pretty in that sundress. You should get out of this house more often."

"Thank you for the compliment," she replied. "What else is going on around town?"

He sat at the table as she continued to unpack and put away the food. "Mayor Jim Burns is pressuring all the businesses on Main Street to update and renovate their shops, and some people aren't happy about it. Former mayor Frank Kean is buzzing around between town and the construction site for the new park, and Claire Silver and Bo McBride got engaged."

He slapped his hand over his mouth, his eyes wide. "Maybe I shouldn't have told you that last part."

Savannah smiled. "No, it's okay. I hope he and Claire will be very happy together." She wasn't surprised they had found love together, and she wanted love for Bo. He would always hold a special place in her heart as the man who had once loved Shelly.

"You know, maybe we could go out some time," Chad said. "Maybe have dinner at the café. You know, just casual-like." His gaze moved from her to the stove and then back to her.

"I'm sorry, Chad. It's nothing personal, but I don't go out."

He frowned. "Are you sure it's nothing personal? I know I don't have a great job, and I'm not as smart as a lot of people."

"It has nothing to do with that, and I think you're very smart," she quickly replied. "I think you're very nice. It has nothing to do with you, Chad. I just don't go out with anyone."

Chad appeared satisfied with her answer. He stayed until the last food item had been put away, and then he left. She'd had a feeling that he had a crush on her, but she never played to it.

All she really knew about him was that he worked for his mother, Sharon, at the grocery store and lived in a small apartment in the back of the store. He was a pleasant-looking man, but he was a bit slow.

Today had been the first time he'd actually asked her out. She hoped she hadn't hurt his feelings by turning him down.

Dismissing those thoughts, she focused all her attention on pulling out the ingredients she needed to make Cajun skillet fillets. There was nothing better than beef fillets and shrimp paired with a special blend of blackening spices and lobster stock. She decided to cook a side of fresh asparagus in garlic and butter.

The only time she allowed any happiness to fill her heart, to seep into her soul, was when she cooked. All of her thoughts, all of her energy went into the food.

There were many times Sharon special-ordered items for her because the local store didn't carry much in the way of specialty foods.

It didn't take long for the kitchen to fill with a variety of wonderful scents. It brought back the times that Savannah's mother had cooked delicious meals for the family. She was always experimenting and tweaking recipes and was responsible for Savannah's love of cooking.

She cooked two steaks and a dozen shrimp, deciding that she'd eat the second portion the next night… the night she walked for the last time as Shelly's ghost.

It was six o'clock and everything was ready for plating when the doorbell rang. She nearly jumped out of her skin. She couldn't remember the last time she'd heard the chime indicating somebody was at the front door.

She looked out the peephole to see Josh on the front porch. Had he changed his mind about giving her tomorrow night? She opened the door, and he greeted her with the sexy smile that twisted her heart in an uncomfortable way.

"What a surprise," she said as she opened the door to allow him inside.

"Since it was one of my nights off, I just thought I'd

stop by and check in before tomorrow night," he said. "Hmm, something smells terrific."

"It's dinner. I was just about to put it on a plate."

"Smells like a lucky plate," he replied.

She thought of the two steaks and the dozen shrimp. "Are you hungry? I have plenty if you'd like to join me."

His eyes lit with pleasure. "I'd love to join you."

As he followed her into the kitchen, she wondered what in the world had possessed her to invite him to dinner. She told herself the reason was that she had to play nice with him until after tomorrow night, and then she wouldn't have to play with him at all.

She gestured him to a seat at the table as she moved to the cabinet to get down another plate. She didn't know what to say. She'd forgotten how to make small talk. It was a surprising revelation.

"I assume you've had a quiet week," he finally said, breaking what had grown into an awkward silence.

"I always have quiet weeks." She filled two glasses with iced tea and added them and silverware to the table, then returned to the stove to put the food on the plates. "What about you?"

He leaned back in the chair, looking relaxed, as if he belonged there. "Let's see. On Monday night I got a call of an intruder in the attic of Mildred Samps's house. It turned out to be a raccoon that had gotten in through a hole in the eaves. I called out Chase Marshall from Fish and Game, and he managed to get the creature out."

"Tell me more," she said as she focused on plating

the food in a visually pleasing way. She'd much rather listen to him talk than have to talk herself.

"On Tuesday night I was called out to Jimmy's Place to break up a fight between two drunks."

She glanced at him in surprise. "Jimmy doesn't usually let things get out of control like that, and I still think of it as Bo's Place."

"Bo definitely had a flair for bringing in a crowd when he owned it. Jimmy doesn't have Bo's natural charisma. Anyway, that brings us to last night, when there were no calls and I just drove up and down the streets for hours. Working the night shift in this town isn't all that challenging."

"I'm sure there are times when a good deputy is necessary after dark. Isn't that when bad things happen?" She delivered the plates to the table.

"Jeez, it all looks too pretty to eat. Do you cook like this every night?"

She sat at the table across from him and shook her head. "Usually just on my nights off."

"That's right. I just remembered that you went to culinary school in Jackson. Didn't I hear somewhere that you were going to open a restaurant at one time?"

"That was another lifetime," she replied. "Dig in while it's warm."

He cut into the steak and took a bite. "This is amazingly delicious. You should put opening that restaurant in this lifetime."

She felt the warmth of a blush creep into her cheeks, along with a flush of pleasure that swept over her at his words, but it lasted only a moment. "I don't have the passion I once had for cooking for other people."

He popped a shrimp in his mouth and chased it with a drink of tea. He gazed at her curiously. "So, what do you have a passion for these days?"

"Keeping Shelly's memory alive." The one thing he was taking away from her. "Besides, as far as I'm concerned, passion is vastly overrated," she added. "What about you? What do you feel passionate about?"

"My job, this town and the people I serve," he answered easily.

"What about a girlfriend?" She was just curious. She certainly didn't care one way or the other whether he had a girlfriend or not.

"Nobody special. Although I'm ready to find the woman who will be by my side for the rest of my life, the woman who will give me some kids, and we'll all live happily ever after." He laughed. "I sound like a woman whose biological clock is ticking."

His words brought a smile to Savannah's lips. "You sound like a man ready to move into a new phase of life."

He stared at her. "You should do that more often. I'd forgotten how you look when you smile."

"Eat your dinner," she replied as a new warmth filled her. She was ready for him to leave. He confused her. He made her feel uncomfortable. He had no place at her table, and she had been impulsive in inviting him in.

He seemed attuned to her discomfort. He ate quickly and didn't ask her any more questions but rather kept up an easy monologue about his work, the new amusement park and the changes that were already happening in the town.

When they'd finished eating, she insisted he not help with the cleanup but instead hurried him toward the front door. "Thanks for the unexpected meal," he said. His eyes had gone dark blue like deep, unfathomable waters.

"No problem," she replied. Away from the kitchen with all its cooking scents, she could smell his cologne and remembered the brief moment of being held in his arms while she wept in the tunnel.

"Then we're still on for tomorrow night?" he asked.

"Definitely. We'll meet at the bush in the backyard at around eleven thirty or so tomorrow night."

"Then I'll see you tomorrow night."

She breathed a sigh of relief as she closed and locked the door behind him. She sank into a nearby chair, the scent of him still filling her head.

There had been a time when she'd been certain he was going to ask her out, and there had been a time when she'd desperately hoped he would. He'd been the one man in town who had managed to quicken her heartbeat at the mere sight of him.

They had flirted outrageously with each other whenever they were together in a group. Shelly had teased her unmercifully about her crush on Josh.

But that had been before life had kicked her so hard she didn't want to play anymore. She'd picked up her marbles and crawled into a cave where she felt safe and secure, a place where no more hurt could touch her again.

She got up from the chair and went back into the kitchen to clear the dishes from the table and clean up the rest of her cooking mess, dismissing any more thoughts of Josh.

She slept late the next morning, as was her custom with her night job, and spent most of the afternoon and evening restlessly pacing the floor, cleaning things that were already clean, both anticipating and dreading the night to come.

By eleven o'clock she was in the bathroom, using powder to whiten her face and already clad in her "ghost" costume for the last time.

Tonight she would hear Shelly's name shouted, and after tonight she didn't know if she would ever hear anyone speak of her sister again. It was as if Shelly was dying a second time, and this time it would be final.

By eleven thirty, she was at the bush, waiting for Josh to arrive. She couldn't ignore the aching sadness in her heart and yet also knew that these Shelly walks were a part of her that wasn't quite rational.

She waited impatiently, expecting Josh to show up any moment. But minutes passed, and when she'd waited fifteen minutes, she had to move. She'd warned him that if he wasn't here on time, she'd go it alone, as she had so many times in the past year.

With a final glance around the backyard and no sign of Josh in sight, she slipped down the rabbit hole and turned on her penlight.

Everyone knew that Shelly's "ghost" usually showed up on Friday nights around midnight. She couldn't let down her "fans" by being late. She'd even heard from Chad one time that young teenagers planned slumber parties and included coming to watch for Shelly's ghost as part of the night's activities.

She moved through the tunnel more quickly than usual, all the while listening for the sound of Josh coming down to join her.

Tomorrow this place would probably be crawling with people. Experts of one sort or another would explore all the passageways, try to date the network, and eventually there might even be tours set up by the town, eager to make money off the unexpected find.

She reached the planks that would take her up, surprised that she'd heard nothing to indicate that Josh was somewhere behind her. He'd obviously been held up by something.

She went up the steps and crouched by the trunk of the tree. For a moment the only things she heard were the croak of frogs and the splash of water from the nearby lagoon.

Wouldn't it be ironic if there was nobody hiding behind the bushes tonight, nobody to witness this final tribute to her dead sister? Then she heard them…the giggling and whispering of her audience. Thank goodness she wouldn't make this last walk without anyone to watch.

When she thought it was just around midnight, she turned on the flashlight that gave her the otherworldly glow. She made her walk as cries of her sister's name filled the air.

Shelly. Savannah missed her so badly. Without these walks, Shelly would eventually become completely ir-relevant and forgotten. The fact ached in Savannah's heart.

When she reached the other side, she turned off the light and hurried to the opening of the cave. She disap-peared inside and leaned weakly against the earthen wall of the tunnel.

It was done. It was over. Now the memory of Shelly would remain only in her mind. Perhaps for several weeks, maybe even a month or so, teenagers would gather behind the bushes to see her "ghost," but when no more appearances occurred, eventually they'd find something else to do on their Friday nights.

Turning on her penlight, she then began the trek back to where she'd begun. Weary sadness moved her feet slowly. Her parents rarely spoke to her. She had no relationship with Mac. Now her last link to Shelly had been broken.

She'd been alone for the past two years, but now she felt an emptiness, a depth of loneliness she'd never felt before. *You'll be fine*, a little voice whispered in her head. And she would be okay. She still had her work at the inn and her nights of cooking, and that was all she really needed.

She had three more dark offshoot passageways to go by, and then she'd be home. As she started past the first one, a hand reached out and grabbed her by the arm.

She shrieked in shock and yanked backward. She crashed to the ground, the penlight falling just out of her reach. Panic and terror shot through her as somebody or something grabbed her by the foot and began to drag her into the dark tunnel.

She kicked and clawed the ground in an effort to get away, but whoever had her was strong, and she felt herself being slowly pulled into the blackness of the unknown corridor.

Chapter Four

"You both need to stop this cycle," Josh said impatiently. He glared at the couple seated on a sagging sofa in one of the shanties that stood near the swamp on the west side of town.

Daisy Wilcox sported a split lip, and her husband, Judd, had scratch marks down his cheek. This wasn't the first time Josh had been called here for a domestic situation.

"I should just take you both in, let you spend some time in jail," Josh said, aware that time was ticking by and it was just a few minutes before he was supposed to meet Savannah in her backyard.

"It was just a little lover's spat," Daisy protested and grabbed Judd's hand. "I overreacted and shouldn't have called the sheriff's office. We're fine now. There's no reason to arrest us."

"Yeah, we're cool," Judd said and patted his wife's ample thigh.

The small room reeked of alcohol and pot. Daisy's words were slurred and Judd's pupils were huge. Josh had cause to take them in, but they weren't bad people. They were part of the poor of Lost Lagoon, swamp people who had little hope and tried to escape that hopelessness by masking their pain with whatever was available.

Besides, if he ran them in, there would be paperwork to fill out, processes that needed to be followed. It all took time, and he was aware of every minute that ticked by. In any case, each of them would refuse to press charges against the other, and it would all be a waste of time.

"If I'm called out here again tonight, then you're both going to be arrested," he warned them as he had a dozen times before. "Put the booze and whatever else you're using away and stop this nonsense."

"We will," Daisy replied and leaned into her husband. She smiled up at Judd. "You know I love you, baby."

Judd returned her smile. "Back at you, babe."

Minutes later, as Josh drove to Savannah's house, he thought about the couple he'd just left. About once a month one officer or another was called to the address to respond to a fight.

Usually by the time the officer got there, the fight was over and the two were lovebirds once again. Their injuries were usually superficial and always sported by both. Josh swore to himself that the next time he was called out there, he would make arrests and let the both of them cool their heels in jail and hopefully make them think about abuse and love. Some people just didn't get it. Love wasn't supposed to hurt.

His thoughts quickly shifted to Savannah as he looked at the clock on his dashboard and cursed inwardly. It was midnight. She was probably already making her ghostly walk.

By the time he parked in her driveway and ran to the backyard, he figured he might as well just wait. She should be coming back up at any moment.

Dammit, he'd wanted to take this final walk with her. Even though he thought what she was doing was more than a little bit crazy, he knew tonight's walk would be emotionally difficult for her.

He'd wanted to be by her side. The darkness of her eyes and the obvious emptiness in her life haunted him. He felt partially responsible for how isolated she'd become, for the obvious grief that still ate at her.

He had so many memories of the laughing, flirting Savannah who had stirred his senses, a woman he'd wanted desperately. He wanted to find that woman again, to help her heal not just for herself, but for him. Time hadn't erased his desire for her.

Would things have been different for her if he'd pushed Sheriff Trey Walker in the investigation of Shelly's murder? If the case had been closed and the killer was behind bars, would that have given Savannah the closure she needed to move forward in a meaningful way?

The problem was, she had nobody to offer her support and encouragement. Her parents had left town, and she apparently wasn't close to her brother. Whatever friends she'd possessed had either drifted away or

been shoved away by her, leaving her alone to cope...
and she hadn't coped.

Every muscle in his body stiffened as he thought he
heard a faint cry coming from the hole in the ground.
He turned on his flashlight and shone it down, seeing
nothing but earth.

Had he heard her crying? Weeping because she
knew this was the end of her walks? Should he go
down and console her? Or let her cry in private? He
had a feeling that if she was crying, she wouldn't welcome his presence.

He heard her again, only this time instead of weeping, it sounded like a scream of terror. With his gun
in one hand, his flashlight in the other and adrenaline
pumping through his body, he dropped down into the
hole.

The first thing he saw was the penlight beam, shining at him from the floor in the distance. What he didn't
see was any sign of Savannah.

"Savannah!" He yelled her name and it echoed in
the air.

He quickly walked forward, his gun leading the
way and his heart pounding a million beats a minute.
Where was Savannah? Why was her flashlight on the
ground? What in the hell was happening?

"Josh, help!" Her cry seemed to come from all sides
of him. He moved faster, and when he came to the first
entrance of an offshoot tunnel, he spun to shine his
flashlight and gun down into the darkness.

"Savannah," he shouted again.

"I'm here." Her voice came again. He shone his light back up the main tunnel and saw her crawling out of one of the offshoot passageways ahead of him.

He ran toward her, his heart still beating at a dizzying speed. She crawled toward him and began to cry. Before he reached her, she got to her feet and raced toward him, slamming into his chest and holding tightly to him. "Somebody grabbed me," she managed to gasp between sobs. "He tried to drag me down the tunnel."

Josh peeled her away from him. "Get out of here and get into your house. I need to check it out."

She grabbed his arm. "Be careful." She quickly turned and hurried toward the exit. Josh shone his light on her until he saw her leave the tunnel. Then he turned around and headed forward.

Every nerve, every sense he possessed tingled with hyperawareness as he approached the passageway where, according to Savannah, somebody had jumped out and grabbed her.

He didn't even want to think about how frightened she'd been, how filthy she'd looked and how helpless she'd appeared crawling along the floor out of the unexplored tunnel.

When he reached the place she'd crawled out of, he shone his light to illuminate the utter blackness of the underground. Nothing. He couldn't see anything as far as his flashlight beam could reach.

Tightening his grip on his gun, he walked down the unfamiliar tunnel. There was nothing to distinguish it from the one he'd just left. He followed it until he came to a fork and didn't know which way to go. Uncertain whether he could find his way back if he ventured too far, he gave up the hunt. Besides, he imagined Savannah's attacker was long gone by now.

He turned back, eager to get to her and find out everything that had happened. Who had been down here? Who would have attacked her? Hopefully she had managed to get a glimpse of whoever had grabbed her.

As he headed toward her house, he checked the yard but saw nothing amiss, nobody hiding in the shadows of night. When he reached the back door, he saw her seated at the table. She got up and unlocked the door to allow him in.

"I didn't see anyone," he said as they both sat down. She looked like hell. Dirt covered her white gown, and the absence of the white makeup she used showed in the tiny trails of her tears. Her eyes still held the haunting vestiges of horror.

He reached across the table for one of her hands. She grasped onto him, hers trembling. "Tell me exactly what happened," he said.

"I waited for you." There was no censure in her slightly breathy voice.

He squeezed her hand a little tighter. "I'm so sorry I wasn't here. I had a domestic call I had to respond to." How he wished he had been by her side. Nobody would have touched her if he'd been down there with her.

She nodded. "I finally went and did my walk, and when I was coming back, somebody from that connecting tunnel reached out and grabbed me by the arm.

I managed to jerk away, but I fell down and lost my penlight."

She paused a moment and drew a deep, tremulous breath. "Then whoever it was grabbed my foot and started to drag me." She looked down at her fingernails. He noticed the dirt beneath them. "I desperately clawed at the ground and kicked as hard as I could, but whoever it was, was strong...too strong for me to get away. As soon as you called my name, he let go of me. Thank goodness you showed up when you did."

"Did you see anything? Get a glimpse of his face?" Josh asked hopefully, but she shook her head.

"He had a bright light shining in my face." She frowned thoughtfully. "I think the light was on a hat."

"You mean like a miner's hat?"

"Yes, like that." She pulled her hand from his and instead wrapped her arms around herself as if chilled to the bone. "I thought he was going to drag me off before you could find me, and nobody would ever know what happened to me. I thought I was the only one who knew about those tunnels, besides you. Why would anyone else be down there? Why would they want to attack me?"

So many questions, and he had no answers for her. "We need to call Trey," he finally said. "It's time he knew not only about the tunnels but also about somebody being down there and assaulting you."

He pulled out his cell phone and made the call to the sheriff, who indicated he'd be there in the next twenty minutes or so.

"He'll think I'm crazy," she said and uncrossed her arms from around herself. "He'll have to know about my ghost walks, and he'll write me off as a nut."

"I won't let that happen, Savannah. I'm not going to let anyone write you off as a nut. I'm on your side." As he should have been two years before.

"I think for the first time in a long time I need somebody on my side," she replied, and as she held his gaze, he swore to himself that he would do whatever possible to find the person responsible for the fear that still shadowed her eyes.

SHE DESPERATELY WANTED to shower. She needed to get the dirt off her body and out from under her fingernails and the last of the white makeup off her face. But Josh insisted she wait until after Sheriff Walker arrived and she spoke with him.

When the doorbell rang, Savannah remained seated at the kitchen table while Josh went to answer the door. She was still shaken to the core. If Josh hadn't heard her scream, if he'd been five minutes later, who knew what might have happened to her? Any thoughts in that direction terrified her.

She sat up a little straighter when Josh came back into the kitchen, followed by Sheriff Walker. Trey Walker was a nice-looking man in his early forties, but she'd always believed he'd let down her entire family by not doing a thorough enough investigation when Shelly had been murdered. He'd been so certain that

Bo McBride had killed Shelly. She believed he'd never really looked at anyone else.

"Are you dressed up for Halloween already?" Trey asked as he entered the kitchen and looked at her. Josh sat next to her, and Trey took the chair across from her.

"No, I'm dressed like Shelly's ghost who walks the night for the amusement of silly teenagers," she replied. She explained to him about pretending to be Shelly's ghost for the last year.

"I've heard about the ghost rumors, but I'm afraid I never caught one of your performances," Trey replied with a touch of amusement. "So, why am I here tonight when I should be at home and in bed?"

"Savannah was attacked," Josh said. "There are tunnels under the town, and she was down there when somebody attacked her."

"Whoa." Trey held up both his hands to stop Josh from saying anything more. "Tunnels under the town? What are you talking about?"

"There's a whole network of tunnels," Savannah said. "I used one to go from my backyard to the edge of the lagoon where Shelly was murdered, but there are a bunch of them down there."

Trey stared at her as if she'd spoken a foreign language. "What are the tunnels for? Where do they go?" he finally asked.

Savannah explained to him that she only knew the one she used and had no idea where the others went. "I thought I was the only one who knew about them until

I told Josh, but obviously I was wrong. Somebody else was down there tonight."

Trey scratched his head as if that might help him absorb the information. "I've never even heard a rumor about tunnels under the ground, and I've lived here all my life."

"I think they're old…really old," Savannah said.

"The whole point of calling you is that somebody attacked Savannah when she was coming back in one of the tunnels from her ghost walk," Josh said, as if impatient that Trey was preoccupied with the tunnels and not focused on the attack that had taken place.

"Okay, let's hear what happened," Trey said.

As Savannah recounted the attack, a cold core built up inside her as she remembered her horror, the shock of realizing not only she was not alone down there, but also somebody had intended to drag her off to someplace unknown.

When she was finished, Trey frowned. "You haven't given me much to go on. You didn't see the person, so you can't identify anyone. Have either of you told anyone about the tunnels besides me?"

"No," they said in unison.

"I intended to tell you about them in the morning, but then things went crazy tonight," Josh said.

"Don't tell anyone else," Trey said. "I need to talk to Mayor Burns, and I don't want a bunch of yahoos going down there before we've had a chance to discuss how to proceed responsibly."

"I'd just like to get my hands around the throat of the person who grabbed Savannah," Josh said with a touch of fervor in his voice.

"Maybe she surprised whoever was down there and he just reacted," Trey offered.

"All he had to do was back away deeper into that tunnel and I would never have seen him," Savannah replied.

"First thing tomorrow morning I'll be here, and you're going to show me exactly where the entrance to the tunnel is," Trey said to Savannah. "Maybe by figuring out where the other tunnels go, we can also figure out who attacked you."

"I want to be here in the morning, too," Josh said.

"You can't work all night and work all day as well," Trey replied.

"I'll be off the clock at seven. If I decide to be here when you go down, it's on my own time and it's my own choice," Josh countered. "I can always catch a nap before my shift tomorrow night."

Trey shrugged. "It's your call." He turned to look at Savannah. "Why don't I plan on meeting you here at nine?"

"That's fine," she replied. It was now out of her hands. The secret had been told, and she was vaguely surprised to realize she was a bit relieved that she had little or no control over what happened next.

Once the sheriff had left, Savannah also realized she wasn't quite ready to be alone. "Would you mind hanging around long enough for me to take a shower?" she asked.

"Of course. I'll hang around as long as you need me," he replied.

"Feel free to make some coffee or get anything else you want to drink." She got up from the table, eager to get beneath a spray of hot water. She felt as if the tunnel dirt had burrowed into her very soul. The touch of a stranger who meant her harm clung to her and needed to be washed away.

"I'm good. I usually meet Daniel Carson at George's Diner around three thirty, and we grab a cup of coffee together," he said, speaking of a fellow officer who worked the night shift as well.

"You should be able to meet him as usual," she replied. "I shouldn't be long." She got up from the table and headed for the master bedroom with its adjoining bath. The bedroom was empty of furniture, but she often used the bathroom because it was bigger than the one in the hallway.

She set the water in the shower to hot and then climbed out of the filthy gown, untied the flashlight at her waist and took off the white slip she wore beneath.

All the clothing would go into the garbage. Shelly's ghost would walk no more. She adjusted the water so she wouldn't scald herself and then stepped beneath the spray.

She used a small bath brush to scrub the dirt from beneath her nails and then shampooed her hair twice. Each time the horror of those moments in the tunnel tried to take hold, she shoved it back, telling herself it was over now. Josh had gotten to her in time, and there was no reason to be afraid anymore.

And yet the fear didn't seem to get the message that she was now safe. There was no reason to believe the person in the tunnel was specifically after her, no reason to think she was in any more danger.

By the time she finished her shower, she'd managed to distill some of the fear. She noted on the nightstand clock that it was three in the morning. She pulled on her nightgown and a pink cotton robe and then combed her long wet hair and pulled it back with a clip at the nape of her neck.

She found Josh still seated at the table. His eyes lit up at the sight of her. "Feel better?"

"Tons better," she replied.

"Savannah, I'm sorry I wasn't here when you went down into the tunnel."

She offered him a small smile. "Josh, you're a deputy. Trust me, I don't blame you for not being here. You have other responsibilities that come first."

"Still, I should have been here for you." His features displayed his irritation at himself.

"I'd just like to know who was down there and what they were doing."

"Hopefully over the next couple of days we can figure that out." He gazed at her curiously. "How do you feel about no longer doing the ghost walks?"

"Conflicted," she answered honestly. "Someplace in the back of my mind, I knew it had become an unhealthy compulsion, but it helped me keep Shelly relevant…alive. But I meant it when I said tonight was my last walk."

"If you got out more, you'd realize that she's still very relevant. Since Bo has returned to town, he and Claire are asking questions about the night of her death, trying to figure out the truth about what happened that night."

"And what do you think the truth of that night is?" she asked.

"I don't know." He said the words flatly, as if he didn't want to talk about it.

She looked at the clock on the wall. "You'd better get going if you're to meet Daniel at three thirty."

"Are you okay to be here alone?"

"I'm fine now. I'm just ready to go to bed and get a short but good night's sleep before Trey shows up here in the morning." She stood, a deep exhaustion hitting her out of nowhere.

He got up as well, and together they walked to the front door. Before opening it, he turned to face her. "I was just thinking, you gave me a great gourmet meal last night. How about next Thursday night you let me cook for you?"

"Oh, that's not necessary."

"Come on, Savannah. It wouldn't be nice of you not to let me return the favor."

She stared at him. He was so handsome, and there was no question she was drawn to him in a way that was both exciting and frightening. *It's just dinner, for crying out loud*, a little voice whispered in her head.

"Okay," she heard herself agree.

"Great. Why don't we say around six thirty at my place? In the meantime, I'll see you in the morning."

He opened the door, but before he stepped out, he turned back to face her. "You know, tonight wasn't necessarily the end of anything. If you let it, it could be the beginning of a new phase in your life. You don't have to be alone, Savannah."

"I know. Good night, Josh, and thank you for being there when I needed you."

In the back of her mind she wanted to be in his arms. She wanted him to kiss her until she was mindless and no longer had the lingering taste of fear in her mouth. She took a step backward, shocked by her desire.

"Anytime." He hesitated a moment, as if he sensed her desire. His eyes darkened and her breath caught in the back of her throat, but then he turned and went out the door.

She watched him until he reached his car in the driveway, and then she closed and locked the door. She checked the back door to make sure it was secured and then headed for bed.

It was only when she was curled up on her side that she thought of Josh's parting words. What he didn't understand was that she didn't want a new phase in her life. She didn't want a new life at all.

What he didn't understand was that she'd been

blessedly numb in her isolation. What she feared most was that if she stepped out of that isolation, she might feel again, and those feelings would truly drive her into madness.

Chapter Five

It was a restless night for Savannah. She tossed and turned with thoughts of the horrifying attack, her confused feelings about Josh and the knowledge that she would never make a ghost walk again.

She didn't want to, not now that she knew somebody else was also using the tunnels, somebody who had presented a danger to her. In fact, she wouldn't mind a bit if Josh brought in that backhoe and filled in the entrance to the tunnel in her backyard.

As she dressed for the day, she thought about the dinner invitation she'd accepted from Josh. She shouldn't go. She should find some reason to cancel. It was just a bad idea, and yet when she thought of how his features had lit up when she'd finally agreed, she knew she wasn't going to cancel on him.

She'd get through the meal, and then that would be the end of any interaction with Josh. She wasn't interested in a romantic flirtation. She wasn't interested in finding love.

She'd loved her parents, and they had deserted her. She'd loved her brother despite his flaws, but he wanted nothing to do with her. Finally, she'd loved Shelly, and Shelly had been stolen from her. She would never use her heart again. She would never allow her emotions to return to life again.

Dinner and done, she thought as she worked her hair into a single braid down her back. As an afterthought, she slid a pale pink lip gloss over her lips and then left the bathroom.

Josh, Trey and Mayor Burns should be arriving within the next fifteen minutes or so. She poured herself a cup of coffee and sat at the kitchen table to wait for them.

She was going down that tunnel one last time with the men. She had to show Trey Walker exactly where she had been dragged and into what tunnel she might have disappeared if not for Josh's fortuitous appearance.

She was unsurprised when Josh was the first of the men to arrive. He appeared at the back door. His night of work showed in his tired eyes and in the slightly deepened lines on his face.

"Coffee?" she asked in greeting.

"Please," he replied and plopped down in the same chair where he'd always sat before, as if he'd claimed it as his own.

He'd obviously gone home from work and changed clothes before coming here, for he wore a pair of jeans and a dark blue T-shirt that did dazzling things to his eyes.

"You look like you need some sleep," she said as she set the coffee before him and then resumed her seat.

"I'll be all right. I'll get a second wind going, and then later this afternoon I'll catch a nap before heading back in to work at eleven." He took a sip of the coffee and set the cup back on the table.

"I checked in with Trey a little while ago, and he and Mayor Burns are eager to get down into the tunnels. They're bringing ropes and colored chalk to mark the passageways so that none of us gets lost down there."

"I think it would be easy to get lost down there," Savannah replied. "That's why I never veered from the tunnel that took me to the lagoon."

"Did you sleep okay after I left? No nightmares?" he asked.

"No nightmares, but it took me a long time to finally go to sleep. I'm going down with you today."

He looked at her in surprise. "I don't think that's a good idea. Besides, why would you want to go?"

"I'll be perfectly safe with the three of you men, and I think I need to go back to banish the memory of the bogeyman."

He raised a dark brow. "So, you did have nightmares."

"No, I just had a hard time getting things out of my mind. I need to go back down there one more time, Josh. I know I'll be safe with all of you there, and it will get last night out of my mind."

"Okay, if it will help, then you'll make us a four-man team." He took another drink of his coffee and sat up straighter in his chair. "I have to admit, I'm more than a little excited to see where all the tunnels lead. And we need to catch the guy responsible for the attack on you last night."

"What I don't understand is this. If he just wanted to scare me, he did that when he grabbed my arm. It was obvious I was terrified, and all I wanted to do was get away. Why did he grab my foot and try to drag me farther into that unknown tunnel?"

Josh's eyes darkened and narrowed. "That's the most important thing to figure out. Who else is using those tunnels and for what purpose? If we can find the answer to those questions then we'll know who attacked you."

"And then I want that tunnel entrance in the backyard filled in so that nobody can climb in or out of that hole ever again," she exclaimed fervently.

At that moment the doorbell rang. Savannah got up to answer. Ten minutes later she and the three men stood at the bush in her backyard. "It's about a three-foot drop, and then the tunnel descends quickly to allow a person to stand," she explained.

As she gazed down the hole where she had descended so many times in the past year, a shiver ran up her spine. She couldn't stop thinking of the night before.

Josh stepped closer to her, as if he'd felt her shiver and somehow wanted to banish it. Sheriff Trey Walker held several lengths of nylon rope, and Mayor Jim Burns had a box of sidewalk chalk in a variety of colors. They all carried high-beam flashlights.

Burns was dressed in a lightweight dark suit and a

white shirt. He had been mayor for less than a year, unseating Mayor Frank Kean, who had served the community in the position of mayor for twelve years.

Jim Burns was younger and had been responsible for the amusement park buying land and building in Lost Lagoon. He was also ambitious, high-strung and more than a little bit arrogant.

Savannah was surprised he hadn't brought his protégé and butt-kisser, city councilman Neil Sampson, with him. She was also surprised that Trey had come without his lapdog, Deputy Ray McClure, a creep who seemed to get away with as little work as possible.

Burns took off his jacket and carefully laid it on the ground, all the while nearly dancing with excitement. "I couldn't believe it when Trey told me about the tunnel system this morning. Let's get to it."

He was the first to descend, followed by Trey. Josh gestured for Savannah to go next, and then he brought up the rear. Instantly she felt a claustrophobia she'd never experienced before as more flashbacks from the night before ran through her head.

"You said this main tunnel runs straight to the lagoon?" Mayor Burns asked.

"Yes, but there are seven or so offshoots between here and there," Savannah replied. "The third one was where I was attacked."

Trey turned back to Josh. "But you checked that tunnel last night and didn't find anything?"

"I followed it until I came to a fork and then wasn't

sure which one to follow, so I came back," Josh explained.

"I think we need to proceed methodically," Burns replied. "We'll start with the first offshoot we come to."

Savannah bit back her disappointment. She'd hoped to follow the tunnel she'd been dragged into to see where it led. Even if there were forks, they could have explored where each one led.

They started down the first offshoot. Trey began to trail the thin rope as they walked, like leaving breadcrumbs for them to follow back home.

Flashlight beams danced on the walls, on the floor and ahead of them as they moved in silence. She had a feeling Trey and Jim were silent with awe. She couldn't help her own curiosity and was aware of the comfort of knowing that Josh had her back.

When they reached another tunnel on the left, Jim pulled out a piece of yellow chalk. As they walked down that way, he marked their path with bright yellow arrows.

Savannah had an unusually good sense of direction; it was what had guided her down the tunnel to the lagoon in the first place. She sensed that this new underpass was taking them someplace in the center of town.

They'd walked for quite some time, stopping every couple of yards for Jim to mark the wall, when they finally came to the end of the tunnel and a set of stairs that led upward.

Savannah's heart began to beat too fast as she wondered where the stairs would lead them. Was this where

her attacker might have come from? Trey shoved the
mayor behind him and pulled his gun. A glance backward showed her that Josh also had his gun out of his
holster.

Had it been out the entire time he'd been walking
behind her? Was he intent on protecting her from anyone who might come up behind them?

She chided herself. It wasn't about her. Certainly protecting the mayor of the city would be uppermost in
Trey's and Josh's minds.

At the top of the stairs was an old wooden trap door
in the ceiling. Trey shoved it open about an inch, just
enough to allow in a faint glow of daylight.

"Where does it go?" Jim asked in a whisper.

"I'm not sure. I won't know where we are until we
go up." He shoved the door open farther, but held it so
that it wouldn't make any noise when it fell to whatever floor it was in.

Trey stepped up first and then the others followed.
Savannah immediately suspected where they were…in
the storeroom in the back of Mama Baptiste's Apothecary Shop. The smell of herbs and spices, of mysterious roots and such filled the air.

Trey closed the door quickly, and Savannah noted
that it seemed to disappear as it fit so neatly into the
dusty wood floor. It would be easy for nobody to know
it was there.

Trey held up his finger to silence anyone from
speaking while wild thoughts flew through Savan-

nah's head. There was no way it had been Mama Baptiste down in the tunnel the night she'd been attacked.

But what about Mama Baptiste's son, thirty-three-year-old Eric? He and Shelly had shared a friendship of sorts before her death, but Savannah had always found the dark-haired, black-eyed man to radiate a dangerous energy.

Was it possible that he'd been the person to attack her? And if so, why? And if he had some reason to want to hurt her, would he come after her again?

Mama Baptiste squealed in surprise as the four of them came out of her storage room. She clasped a hand to her chest. "Most of my customers use the front door instead of the back, and they don't come in with guns drawn," she exclaimed.

Josh put his gun back in his holster, as did Trey. Mama's store held walls of tourist-type items for sale, but her main business was the herb and root concoctions she mixed and sold to people in town who suffered everything from an upset stomach to arthritis.

Strange herbs and roots hung drying from rafters in the ceiling, and Mama herself looked part gypsy with her long salt-and-pepper hair wild down her shoulders. She was clad in a bright red peasant-style blouse and a floor-length red-and-yellow floral skirt.

"We didn't use the back door," Jim said.

Mama Baptiste frowned in confusion. "Then how did you get in?"

"Through a tunnel that led to a trap door in the floor in your storage room," Trey said.

Josh watched Mama's face intently. She appeared genuinely shocked. "What are you talking about? A door in my floor?"

"Come on. I'll show you." Trey disappeared into the back room with Mama Baptiste as Mayor Burns wandered away from where Savannah and Josh stood near the counter.

"What about Eric?" Savannah asked softly.

"Have you and he had any problems?" Josh asked.

"None. I know he and Shelly were friendly, at least as much as Eric is friendly with anyone, but he and I have never had much interaction," Savannah replied.

"I swear I didn't know that hole in the floor was there," Mama Baptiste said as she and Trey returned from the back room.

"Maybe we should speak with Eric," Josh said. "Is he around?"

"I'm not sure where he is," Mama replied. She walked behind the counter and picked up a cell phone. "I can call him and get him here. But what does a tunnel have to do with Eric?"

"We'd just like to have a talk with him," Trey said with a sharp gaze at Josh.

Josh tamped down an edge of irritation. God forbid he attempt to do his job, especially when his boss was around. Mama made the call, and while they waited for Eric to arrive, Jim and Trey talked to her about business while Savannah and Josh wandered the aisles of the store.

Savannah said nothing, but Josh sensed a nervous

energy emanating from her, one that he didn't understand given the circumstances of the situation.

He finally took her by the arm and led her to a corner of the store, away from where the others stood waiting for Eric to arrive.

"What's going on? You seem unusually nervous."

Her dark chocolate-colored eyes gazed up at him, and in the depths of them he saw not just anxiety but also confusion. "I was just remembering back to the time before Shelly's murder. She and Eric were spending some time together, and Shelly had told me one night that she had a sticky situation on her hands, but she refused to be specific about what she was talking about."

Josh contemplated her words. "Do you think Eric had something to do with your sister's murder?"

"I don't know who killed Shelly, and I've really not had any interaction with Eric since Shelly's death. He just always made me feel uncomfortable."

"You haven't had much interaction with much of anyone since your sister's death," Josh replied.

"And that's the way I like it," she said firmly.

Josh wanted to tell her that it wasn't right for her to be such a recluse, that she was young and beautiful and deserved a life of happiness. Before he could say any of those things, Eric walked into the shop.

Eric Baptiste had the proverbial bad-boy aura. Clad in black jeans and a short-sleeved black T-shirt, he also had lean features and lips that looked as if they'd never smiled.

He was something of a mystery. He'd been born and raised in Lost Lagoon, but he was a loner who didn't appear to have friends and lived alone in one of the shanties on the swamp side of town.

"What's going on here?" he asked as his gaze went from Trey to Josh.

"Do you know about the tunnel under the floor in the storeroom?" Trey asked.

Eric's eyes narrowed slightly, so slightly that Josh wondered if anyone else noticed. It was a definite tell to Josh what the answer was to the question.

"Yeah, I know about the tunnels," Eric replied. His mother looked at him in surprise.

"Have you been down there?" Trey asked.

"I've used them." He looked at Savannah. "I use the same tunnel you do to get to the swamp."

"Why?" Trey asked.

"It's the easiest way to get to the swamp to gather the herbs and roots that Mama uses in her concoctions."

Savannah moved a bit closer to Josh. "Did you attack me? Did you try to drag me into another tunnel?"

Eric's features expressed genuine surprise. "I'd never hurt you, Savannah." His gaze on her was dark and intense, and Josh fought the impulse to place an arm around her and pull her tight against him.

A softness swept over Eric's face. "I can't believe how much you look like her." He frowned and turned back to face Trey.

"How well do you know the tunnel system?" Trey asked.

"I know there are lots of tunnels, and I also know Savannah and I aren't the only ones who have used them."

"Who else?" Jim asked. "And do you know the network well enough to map it out for us?"

Eric shook his head. "I don't know who else, but several times when I've been down there, I've heard male voices. I tried one night to figure out where they were coming from, but sound is distorted down there, and I never saw anyone else."

"What about mapping the network?" Jim repeated.

Once again Eric shook his head, his shaggy black hair shining in the light dancing through the store's window. "No way. I've only been in a couple of the tunnels. I mostly use the one in the back room to get to the tunnel that Savannah has been using to get to the lagoon."

"So you knew Savannah was using that tunnel," Josh said.

"I knew that she was mostly in the tunnel on Thursday or Friday nights, so I stayed away on those nights," Eric replied.

Once again he looked at Savannah. "If this is about somebody attacking you, then you all need to look someplace else. Shelly and I had become friends before her murder, and I would never hurt Savannah. When I look at her, she reminds me of how much I cared about Shelly."

"Where were you last night around midnight?" Trey asked.

Eric tensed and a knot appeared in his jaw, pulsing

in irritation. "I was at home at midnight last night. Was anyone with me? No, I don't have visitors. Did anyone call me? No, I don't chitchat on my phone at that time of night."

"Then nobody can corroborate your alibi," Trey said.

"My son would never hurt anyone," Mama exclaimed.

"Is this the part where you tell me not to leave town?" Eric asked wryly. "Is that it? Can I go now?"

Trey waved his hand dismissively. Eric nodded to his mother, then to Savannah, and then left the store.

"Everyone in town thinks Eric is just a no-count loner swamp rat who works for his mother in her store," Mama Baptiste said, her dark eyes lit with a fiery glow. "But he has a degree in botany. He could work anywhere he wanted, but he chooses to stay here in a town that gives him no respect, because he loves me. He would never hurt anyone."

"We're done here for now," Trey said.

"We're done for the day," Jim replied and gestured for them to follow him out the front door. "I've got a two-thirty meeting with Rod Nixon and Frank Kean about amusement park business," he said once they were outside in the hot afternoon sun. Rod Nixon was the owner of the amusement park.

Jim looked down at his white shirt that now had the tinge of brown dirt. "I need to get showered and changed. We'll work the tunnels again tomorrow, but in the meantime, I want this all kept quiet, and I don't want anyone down there without me." He turned to

Savannah. "I'll pick up my suit jacket from your place sometime tomorrow."

"I'll walk with you back to the station," Trey said to the mayor. City Hall was located right next door to the sheriff's station. "Josh, go home and get some sleep. Savannah, I'll be in touch if I learn anything new about the attack."

Together the two men headed down the street, and Josh turned to Savannah. "Come on, I'll walk you home."

"That's not necessary," she protested. "You need to get to bed so that you can be alert for your night shift."

"A few extra minutes won't matter, and besides, I insist," he replied.

They walked down the sidewalk that would take them to the side street that would eventually lead to her house. "I can't believe that Eric was using the same tunnel I've been using for so long and I never knew," she said.

"You know that makes him our number one suspect in the attack on you," Josh replied.

"But he said he'd heard other voices down there, which means somebody else is using the tunnels," she protested.

"That's what he said."

"You don't believe him?"

Josh released a tired sigh. "At this point I don't know what to believe. All I know is that I didn't like the way Eric looked at you or that he said you look so much like Shelly."

Somewhere in the back of his mind, Josh knew his feelings for Savannah weren't just professional. It was a touch of personal jealousy that had winged through him as he'd seen the soft look Eric had given her.

"Are you implying that Eric might have killed Shelly? I certainly didn't hear his name mentioned during the investigation." There was a touch of censure in her voice.

"We didn't know about any connection between Eric and Shelly at the time," he replied. A knot formed in his stomach, as it always did when he thought of the sloppy investigation into Shelly's murder.

They turned off onto the side street. "All I know is that I think it would be a good idea for you to keep your distance from Eric."

"I keep my distance from everyone," she replied wryly. "The only person I see on a regular basis is Chad Williams, who delivers groceries to me once a week, and my neighbor, who wishes I'd move out."

"Jeffrey Allen?"

She nodded. "I think he was thrilled when my parents left town, but he was upset that they left the house to Mac and me. He was hoping he would finally be able to buy it. He's rude and hateful and has made it clear that he thinks I should move out and sell the house."

"Has he given you any indication that he knows about the tunnels?"

"No, but I'm sure he probably knows about the one in my backyard now since we all went down it this morning. I imagine he was at his back window watching everything. There isn't much he misses in the neighborhood."

"Maybe you just gave me a second suspect to add to the short list," Josh said.

"I don't know. He's a creep but I can't imagine him going to such a length as attacking me to get me to move out."

By that time they'd reached her house. She pulled a small key ring from her back pocket and unlocked her front door, then turned back to face him. "Thanks for the company. Now go home and go to bed."

"You'd better do the same. You have a night shift to work tonight, too."

"True, but I can doze on my night shift. You have to be alert and ready to fight crime at any moment."

"If I don't see you before, I'll see you Thursday night at my place for dinner. Around six thirty?"

She hesitated, and he sensed she was about to cancel on him. He didn't want that to happen. He knew that she was forever changed by the murder of her sister and the basic destruction of her family, but he also knew she dwelt in a dark place that had become far too comfortable for her.

"I've already bought the best steaks in town and can't wait to get your opinion on my special seasoning," he said hurriedly.

She nodded, albeit with obvious reluctance. "Then I'll see you Thursday night."

"Great," he replied.

Minutes later as he headed toward home, pleasure

filled him at the anticipation of Thursday night, but it was tempered by concern about the attack on her.

Did Eric entertain some kind of sick obsession with Shelly that had now transferred to Savannah? Had he been the one who had attacked her? Or were there really other people using the tunnels? And for what purpose?

Was it possible that something evil was going on beneath the streets of Lost Lagoon?

Chapter Six

Josh felt as if he were preparing for the first date he'd ever had in his life. He awoke about noon and laid out the frozen steaks to thaw, then immediately set to cleaning the house as if a dignitary was coming to visit.

A nervous energy filled him, definitely because he would be spending time alone with Savannah. They wouldn't be traipsing through tunnels or talking to local officials. It would just be the two of them over dinner.

He desperately wanted the night to go well. He wanted the conversation to flow light and easy and for her to feel comfortable in his presence.

They would be eating in his kitchen rather than the formal dining room, which had become his home office. The top of the fine mahogany dining room table was currently covered with a large piece of poster board on which he'd been attempting to map the tunnels.

The kitchen was cozier anyway, he told himself. The round oak table would be conducive to a more intimate setting.

He was in the process of wrapping potatoes in aluminum foil to go into the oven when Daniel Carson opened his back door and walked in. "Don't you look domestic," he said in amusement. "All you're missing is a frilly apron."

"Just making sure I have everything under control," Josh replied. He gestured his fellow deputy and friend to a chair at the table. "Want something to drink?"

"I wouldn't turn down a cold beer," Daniel replied.

Josh snagged two bottles from the fridge and then sat across from Daniel. "So, what's the news of the day?"

"I had breakfast at the café this morning and heard that May Johnson's son is in the hospital from a dope overdose. It was apparently meth."

Josh raised a brow. "We don't get much of that around here. How's he doing?"

"He'll survive. How goes the underworld?"

"I'm not sure I understand why Jim decided to change courses and start in the tunnels closest to the swamp rather than those closest to Savannah's backyard, but we've been down there three times in the last week and have managed to map out a single branch with several forks."

"Anything exciting found?" Daniel asked and then took a swig of his beer.

"Dirt and more dirt. No gold coins, no rubies or diamonds or pirate treasure, just dirt and a couple of exits."

"Exits where?"

"One came up in the floor of one of the abandoned shanties on the swamp side of town, and another one opened up in a pile of brush just outside of town." Josh paused to sip his beer. "We haven't found any sign that those tunnels have been used in recent times."

"Shouldn't they call in some kind of expert for this?" Daniel asked.

"I imagine Mayor Burns eventually will, but I swear right now he's like a kid with a new adventure to explore. He doesn't seem inclined to share the information about the tunnels just yet."

"It is pretty amazing that they've been there all this time and nobody ever knew," Daniel replied. He leaned back in his chair and looked around the kitchen, then focused his attention back on Josh.

"You realize a steak dinner isn't going to make you feel less guilty about what happened two years ago," he said.

"That's not what tonight is about," Josh protested. "She fed me a gourmet meal last week, and so I'm just returning the favor."

"You know I feel guilty, too, about how the investigation into Shelly Sinclair's death went down, but we both knew we'd be risking our jobs if we tried to buck Trey's assessment of the murder. If we'd done anything differently we would have been fired and nothing would have been different anyway."

"I just wonder how different Savannah's life might have been for the last two years if we'd gotten the job done right," Josh admitted.

"I don't want you going all savior on me and trying to save Savannah from herself and in the meantime getting hurt."

"I just think she needs a friend right now."

"Yeah, but the real question is, does she *want* a friend right now?" Daniel countered.

The question hung in Josh's mind long after Daniel had left. Was he trying to assuage his guilt by attempting to build a relationship with Savannah? Or was he simply on a misguided quest to find the woman who had once made his heart beat just a little bit faster, a woman he'd wanted to pursue before tragedy struck?

It didn't matter that he wasn't sure of the answer. All he knew was that he was looking forward to the evening. By the time six twenty had arrived, he was dressed in a pair of jeans and a button-up short-sleeved blue-and-silver-striped shirt.

The table was set. The potatoes were cooking. The steaks were seasoned, and a fresh salad was in the fridge. The only thing missing was his date, and she should be arriving within the next fifteen minutes.

He had called her last night to confirm tonight but had gotten the impression that if there had been a graceful way for her to back out, she would have taken it. But he hadn't given her a chance.

He'd tucked in his shirt twice and opened a bottle of wine when the doorbell rang. He hurried to answer, and when he opened his door, he nearly lost his breath to the beauty of the woman before him.

Clad in a peach-colored sundress that displayed her

beautiful shoulders, her small waistline and the length of her legs, she looked gorgeous.

It was obvious she'd taken extra time and trouble with her appearance. Her lashes looked longer and darker, a faint blush colored her cheeks and her hair fell in soft waves around her shoulders. The only things missing were a smile and a light of anything in her eyes.

"Are you going to invite me in?" she finally asked.

"Oh yeah, of course." He opened the door farther to allow her entry into his hallway. As she passed him, he smelled the floral scent that stirred him on every level.

"Your home is beautiful," she said as she entered the living room. It was furnished with modern but comfortable black-and-white furniture and glass-topped end and coffee tables.

"Let me give you the full tour," he said. She followed him down the hallway, where he showed her the two guest bedrooms, a guest bath and then the master suite complete with the bathroom with the oversized tub. He knew his pride was obvious, but he couldn't help it.

"You have wonderful taste," she said.

"You might change your mind when you see the formal dining room." He led her into the room filled with a desk, computer equipment, file cabinets and the table covered with the poster board of the mapped tunnels.

"You're mapping the tunnels," she said, stating the obvious.

"I'm doing the best I can with the information Trey gives to me. As you can see by the new red and green lines, they've fully explored two more tunnels in the last couple of days, although nothing extraordinary has been found. But we're not talking about that tonight." He gestured her to follow him into the kitchen.

She gasped in surprise as she saw the built-in double oven and an upscale microwave and convection oven. "Do you do a lot of cooking?" she asked as he gestured her to a chair at the table.

"Nah, I occasionally use one of the ovens, but the microwave and my barbecue pit are my real friends. The brick pit on the back patio even has a place for pizza baking. Wine?"

"Okay," she agreed. "Why would you go to the expense to put in such a kitchen when you don't cook?"

"Resale value," he replied. He set a crystal stem of red wine next to the red-and-black dishware that adorned the table. "I think my builder probably took advantage of me in adding all this stuff, especially since I have no desire to sell or move anywhere else."

"It's a dream kitchen," she replied, and for the first time since she'd arrived, her eyes lit with pleasure. "Is there anything I can do to help?" she asked when he took a salad from the refrigerator and placed it in the center of the table.

"Just tell me how you like your steak. Mooing, medium or well-done?"

She laughed. It was a brief noise like a wind chime musically dancing with a sudden breeze. It lasted only a mere second and appeared to surprise her as much as it pleased him.

"I'm sorry. I've never heard rare described as 'mooing' before," she said.

"Don't apologize for laughing, Savannah. If I had the ability, I'd make you laugh as often as possible."

Her eyes went dark. "Medium rare, that's how I like my steak." She focused on her wine and took a sip.

He'd stepped over the line. He picked up the plate with the seasoned steaks. "I'm going to throw these on the grill. I'll be right back." He stepped out the back door, where the elaborate brick grill was hot and ready to cook the meat.

He placed the steaks on the grill and then went back inside. "I'll need to go back out and turn them in just a few minutes."

"Tell me about the special steak rub you use," she said.

"Ah, it's an old family secret," he replied as he leaned a hip against the counter.

"But you're going to share that secret with me," she said with a small curve of her lips.

Hell, if he were a CIA agent, he'd spill every secret he knew for one of her rare, beautiful smiles. "I suppose I am. It's a little bit of molasses, a little bit of bacon and a pinch of cayenne pepper."

"Hmm, sweet with a little kick."

He grinned at her. "Reminds me of somebody I know."

That earned him a genuine smile. "I don't know how sweet I am, but I definitely have a kick."

All too quickly the steaks were done and the meal

was on the table. The conversation revolved around cooking as she shared some of her favorite recipes and he told her about his botched attempts to do any real cooking.

Those stories made her laugh several times. It was sweet music to his ears and confirmed to him that someplace inside the shell she presented to the world was a vibrant young woman who deserved a better life than the one she'd committed herself to.

"Let me help with the cleanup," she said when they finished the meal.

"Nonsense, I have all night to take care of it. How about we take a glass of wine into the living room and talk a little bit more?"

"Okay," she agreed.

He'd noticed her relaxing as the night had progressed, and the fact that she agreed to stay for another glass of wine and a little conversation pleased him.

He carried their wineglasses and followed her into the living room. Instead of sitting on the sofa, she walked over to the bookcase that held keepsakes and photos.

"These are your parents?" she asked and pointed to one of the framed pictures.

"Yeah, those are my folks. They live in Georgia."

"Are you close to them?"

"As close as I can be living this far away," he replied. "I talk to them about twice a week. They come and visit on their anniversary, and I always go home for Christmas."

She pointed to another photo and looked at him in surprise. "Is that you? And do you have a twin brother?"

"Yes, and I did have a twin brother. He died in a car accident when we were fifteen."

She picked up the photo and sank down on the sofa, and he noticed that her hands trembled slightly. She looked up at him, and her eyes were shiny with tears. "How did you manage to survive?"

He sat next to her. "I took his death hard, but I knew I had to go on if for no other reason than to honor him in my heart. That sports car I have is a car Jacob and I dreamed of owning when we were young. We both wanted to be cops when we grew up, and so here I am wearing a deputy's star. I survived, Savannah, and I went on to live my life because it was the only thing I knew how to do."

THE KNOWLEDGE THAT he'd lost a twin brother nearly stole her breath away. For just a moment she forgot about her own losses. She wanted to hold him, to comfort him for the tragedy in his own life.

"I'm so sorry." She didn't even realize she'd slipped her hand into his until she felt the warmth of his wrapping around hers.

"Thanks. It was a long time ago. Sometimes bad things happen to good people, but you already know that."

She set the picture on the coffee table. "Tell me about him."

He smiled. "Jacob was two minutes older than me,

and he never let me forget it. He was definitely the dominant twin. I was a bit shyer, and I idolized him." His smile drifted away.

"That's the way it was between me and Shelly," she replied. "She was only a year older than me, but she was more social and outgoing than me. I idolized her, too. But I was always Shelly's little sister to most of the people in town."

"Just like for the first fifteen years of my life I was Jacob's twin. It took me a while to figure out who I was without him."

She stood and took the picture and returned it to where it belonged. When she returned to the sofa, she took a sip of her wine and eyed him over the rim of the glass. "How did you do it, Josh?" she asked when she'd lowered the glass.

"I just figured the best way to honor Jacob was to live well. I had to find out who I was alone, and that meant just moving forward."

"I should get home," she said abruptly. The night had been too pleasant, his company both relaxing and exciting. Now knowing they shared common tragedies only pulled her emotionally closer to him, and she needed to get away from him.

"It's still early," he protested. "At least finish your wine."

She shook her head, stood and grabbed her purse next to her. "Thanks, but I've had enough wine." He jumped up off the sofa, and she headed for the front door. She turned back to him. "Thank you for a lovely meal, and I think that makes us even where dinner is concerned."

He stepped closer to her, and her heart jumped up in rhythm at his nearness. He smiled, that sexy expression that always pulled a pool of heat into her stomach.

"I don't think we should keep score on dinners," he said teasingly. The light in his eyes darkened, and he reached out and took hold of her chin. "I never saw you as Shelly's sister. You were always sweet, sexy Savannah to me."

Before she knew his intention, his lips captured hers. She wanted to pull away, but his mouth was oh so warm and inviting. Instead of stepping back, she found herself leaning into him, opening her mouth to allow him to deepen the kiss.

She'd once dreamed of what it might be like to be kissed by Josh Griffin, but now she knew her wildest dreams had simply been pale imitations of the real thing. There was no way she could have dreamed of the magic and the fire in his kiss.

She wanted to melt into his arms and stay there forever, and that was what made her break the kiss and step back from him. "I've got to go," she said, needing to escape before she fell into his arms again.

He stepped back from her. "Savannah, find yourself again. Find the person separate from Shelly."

She didn't tell him goodbye. She raced out the door

to escape not just her desire for him, but also his parting words.

She kept her mind carefully schooled to blankness as she drove the short distance home. It was only when she was in bed that she mulled over the night.

There was no question that she'd enjoyed his company. He'd made her laugh for the first time in years, and for the most part, their conversation had been relatively light and easy. He was still the man she'd found sexy and fun two years ago. He was still a man who drew her to him despite her desire to the contrary.

The fact that he'd lost somebody so close to him and had become the man he had spoke of his inner strength, a strength he didn't understand she didn't possess.

Shelly had been the strong one. Her parents had known it. Mac had known it. Everyone had known that Shelly was special, that she was a leader. Savannah had been happy to be in Shelly's shadow.

She tried to think about everything but that kiss. The kiss that had rocked her back on her heels and pulled forth a powerful emotion that had stunned her.

It was the thought of that kiss that finally got her out of bed around one. Sleep eluded her. She went into the kitchen and put the teapot on to boil water. Hopefully a cup of hot tea would relax her enough to sleep.

She pulled down a cup and readied a tea bag and then moved to the kitchen window and stared out into the night. Tomorrow night would be the first time in a long time that she wasn't going to make her ghost walk.

What on earth would she do instead with her night off? She started to move away from the window and then froze. She thought she saw some movement near the back of the yard, where several trees flanked the bush that hid the hole in the ground.

Was there somebody out there? Hiding behind the tree on the left and watching her? Was it Eric Baptiste? Had he been obsessed with Shelly and now had some sort of obsession with her?

She turned off the kitchen light and continued to watch the tree. Had she only imagined somebody out there? Was she just being paranoid?

The whistle from the copper teapot nearly sent her through the ceiling. She cast one more glance out the window and, still seeing nobody, she turned on the light and quickly moved the screeching teakettle off the burner.

Definitely paranoid, she told herself as she fixed her tea and then sat at the table to drink it. There was absolutely no reason to believe that she was somebody's specific target. The attack in the tunnel just might have been a case of being in the wrong place at the wrong time.

She finished her tea and went back to bed, where she finally fell into a deep sleep and dreamed of kissing Josh. When she awakened after noon the next day, her head was still filled with that kiss.

She spent Friday cooking and that evening had a meal of bourbon barbecue pork chops, cheesy corn and homemade biscuits with a touch of jalapeño peppers. She'd just finished eating when Josh called.

"I was wondering if you'd like a little company tonight," he said.

She knew what he was trying to do, fill the hours of the night when she'd normally be anticipating a ghost walk. "That's not necessary, Josh. I'm fine, and I'll be fine through the night."

"I just thought maybe…"

"Really, it isn't necessary," she said firmly. Dinner and done. That was what she had promised herself where he was concerned. "I've appreciated your support, Josh, but there's really no need for you to be worried about me anymore."

She could feel his disappointment even before he spoke. "Oh, okay then. You know I'll be in touch if we get a break in the attack on you in the tunnel."

"Thanks. Then I'll see you around." She hung up quickly, afraid that he might be able to talk her into letting him come over and hang out.

She spent the rest of the evening watching television and then at midnight headed to bed. She had to admit that there was a little bit of relief in not being able to pretend to be Shelly's ghost anymore.

For the first time in a long time, she was eager to go to work on Saturday night. At quarter 'til eleven she got into her car and drove toward the inn. She was grateful to have something to do besides think about her dead sister and a very much alive deputy.

She knocked on the locked front door, and Dorothy Abbott, the older woman who worked the shift before hers, hurried to unlock the door.

"Gonna have a hard time keeping your eyes open tonight," she said as she ushered Savannah inside. "Nobody is checked in. The place is quiet as a tomb." She handed the keys to Savannah. "And now I'm out of here."

The minute Dorothy was out of the door, Savannah relocked it and then headed for the reception desk and settled in for the long night.

She often wondered how Donnie Albright could keep the inn open with so few guests, but she assumed he must have family money and this place was just some sort of tax write-off for him.

She would never have managed to stay in her house if it hadn't been paid off when her parents moved away. Unlike Josh, who had maintained a close relationship with his parents, Savannah rarely heard from hers.

When she did call them, the conversation was strained and uncomfortable. It was as if she was a reminder of things they'd rather forget, a reminder of the daughter they had lost.

It was the same way with her brother, Mac. Since his marriage they'd had little interaction, and when they did it was usually because he wanted to take something out of the house.

Savannah had never been close to Mac and she had come to terms with the desertion of her family, but that didn't make it hurt any less. It only made her miss her sister more.

She pulled a notepad from the desk. It was a regular spiral notebook that she kept here to help her pass the long nights. She not only doodled mindlessly in it but also sometimes worked on recipes she'd like to try. She did this now, using the creative side of her brain to write down ingredients she thought might pair together well and then imagining how they might look on a plate.

The silence was broken only occasionally by thuds or thumps that she assumed were pipes expanding and contracting when the air conditioner turned on and off.

It was just after three when she got up to use the lobby restroom. She washed her hands and then wiped her face with a cold cloth in hopes of getting a second wind. She'd only been here four hours and already felt exhausted by doing nothing.

She stared at her reflection in the mirror over the sink and remembered that darned kiss from Josh. There was no question that he had been attempting to pursue something romantic with her. But she'd made it clear to him last night that she wasn't buying what he was selling.

She just wasn't ready to reenter life. There was still too much grief in her heart to allow in any other emotions. The problem was, Josh's kiss had shown her how to feel again.

Irritated that she was obsessing about a man she

wouldn't invite into her life, she left the bathroom and returned to her chair behind the desk.

She'd just sat down when the lights went out, plunging the inn into utter darkness.

Chapter Seven

Savannah remained frozen. This had never happened before. Had a fuse blown? She was sure the electrical wiring in the building was probably ancient, but she didn't even know where the fuse box was located.

She imagined it was someplace in the basement, but she didn't like to go down there. It was slightly dank and filled with supplies in boxes stacked with no rhyme or reason. Besides, the basement door was located in Donnie's private office.

Even if she found her way to the fuse box in the dark, she wouldn't know what to do when she got there. She knew nothing about electrical issues.

She was just about to reach for the phone to call Donnie when she heard a thump...thump...thump coming down the hallway upstairs. If she'd believed in ghosts, she would have assumed it was the spirit of old Peg Leg walking the hall.

But she didn't believe in ghosts. Whoever it was making the noise was very much human, and starting down the stairs.

"Hello? Who's there?" she asked.

There was no reply, but she could hear the person continuing down the stairs. If it was somebody not to fear, then why hadn't that somebody answered her?

Her heart banged in terror as she slid from her chair and beneath the desk. Who was in here? How had they gotten inside?

Was it possible somebody had sneaked in earlier in the day and had hidden in one of the guest rooms for this moment when she would be here all alone?

"Savannah." The sibilant, gruff, male whisper shot a new tremor of terror through her.

He knew her name. Whoever it was knew she was here, and he obviously wasn't interested in checking into a room for the night. The thumping stopped, and she had a feeling whoever it was had reached the bottom of the staircase.

"You bitch." The voice was guttural and impossible for her to identify. But one thing was clear…whoever he was, he was angry and she was in trouble.

She was a sitting duck under the desk. If he approached any closer she would have no way to escape, nowhere to run or hide.

At the moment the darkness was her friend. She had to assume if she couldn't see him, then he couldn't see her, either. Without making a sound, she scooted out from under the desk and headed in the direction of a large potted plant.

There were several plants in the lobby with pots

large enough for her to crouch behind. Her mind raced with options as she headed toward the closest plant.

She'd just reached the pot when a loud crash came from the direction of the chair she'd been seated in when the lights had first gone out.

She slammed a fist against her mouth in an effort to staunch the scream that begged to be released. She wondered if the noise she had heard when he'd walked across the upstairs had been a baseball bat or some other length of wood that he'd now used to slam into her chair.

Silence.

It was the ominous silence that occurred before an explosion, the proverbial calm before the storm. She tried to make herself as small as possible behind the planter and at the same time listened for any whisper of a sound that would let her know his location.

All of her senses were on fire as terror continued to beat her heart a million miles a minute. Was he close enough to hear her heart? Was he near enough to smell her perfume?

She couldn't smell him. She had no sense of anyone next to her or hovering nearby her. But the darkness of the room made her doubt her ability to sense anything correctly.

"Savannah, you can't hide from me forever." A small flashlight clicked on.

Although the beam of the light let her know he was across the lobby from her, it also shot her terror up a hundred notches. With that flashlight he could hunt her down.

He stood near the sitting area, but his beam of light shot back toward the desk, as if double-checking to make sure he hadn't missed her there.

She couldn't see him in any detail with the light he flashed before him. She couldn't even get a real sense of his height or weight.

Her mind whirled frantically. She couldn't slip into the bathroom. There were no windows, and eventually she'd be trapped in the two-stall room. Her cell phone was in her purse under the desk, so she couldn't call anyone for help. She couldn't even run for the door because it was locked and the keys were in the desk drawer.

The beam of light shone on the opposite side of the lobby, indicating to her that he was methodically checking anywhere that might be a hiding place.

Eventually he'd begin to work this side of the room, and she knew that if he found her, she would never leave the lobby alive. Why? What was this all about? Despite her fear, her brain worked to try to come up with a reason for this happening.

Twice he'd called her by name, making her certain that this wasn't just a random act of violence but rather a targeted attack on her.

She couldn't stay behind the plant pot forever. It was only a matter of minutes before he'd move to this side of the lobby and his light found her.

The effort to keep her screams inside was monumental. If she made any noise at all, he'd get her. She jumped as a crash of pottery splintered the silence.

"I'm going to find you, and you're going to pay for screwing things up." Unbridled rage filled the voice that she somehow knew she should be able to identify, but couldn't.

She was frozen with fear but knew she had to move and move fast. The question was, where? Where could she go where he'd never find her?

Should she try to double back to the desk, where he'd already searched? Could she silently follow him, staying behind where he was heading?

At seven Donnie would be arriving for the day, but that was still hours away. Her chest constricted, and for a moment she thought she couldn't breathe.

Think, her brain commanded. She had to do something before he found her and smashed her skull in with whatever weapon he wielded. The treasure chest! She was tall. She could reach the side and pull herself in. She could bury herself among the oversized jewels and maybe…just maybe he wouldn't think of looking for her in there.

The problem was, in order to reach the treasure chest she'd have to leave her hiding spot and creep across a large open area, where she would be exposed.

Die here behind the plant or die in the middle of the lobby floor? At least if she tried to get to the treasure chest, she'd know she'd done something in an attempt to stay alive.

Holding her breath, she scooted on her butt out from

behind the planter, careful not to make any noise that would draw attention.

As the flashlight beam shot across the other side of the lobby, she could see a faint glimpse of the person holding the light. Unfortunately, the person was dressed all in black and had on a ski mask, making him bleed into the surrounding darkness. She couldn't even begin to identify him.

She continued at a snail's pace across the floor, praying that his light wouldn't find her, that she wouldn't make a sound that would draw his attention.

There was another crash and the splintering sound of pottery shattering. He'd apparently smashed another plant pot. His destructive rage terrified her.

She finally made it to the side of the treasure chest where she could no longer see him, which meant he couldn't see her. If she climbed into the structure, would he find her there? If he did, she was aware that she was placing herself in a spot where there would be no escape.

She had no other choice. Within minutes or even seconds she would be out of options. She slid up to her feet and turned to grasp the top of the treasure chest.

Praying that she didn't grunt or groan, that she had the strength to pull herself up and into the chest, she drew a deep breath for courage and then pulled herself up.

The chest was filled with papier-mâché and Styrofoam rubies and emeralds, diamonds and coins. She managed to get into the chest and then burrowed down amid the fake jewels. She was grateful that when she buried herself, her attacker smashed another pot, hiding whatever sound she made as she covered herself with the large baubles.

"When I find you, I'm going to smash your head in," he growled.

She fought against a shiver and once again placed a hand over her mouth to staunch her need to cry, to scream out loud in horror. Why? Who was this man who wanted her dead, and what was his reason?

What time was it? How long would he carry on this attack? Aside from the abject terror that blazed through her, she felt claustrophobic as she burrowed deeper toward the bottom of the chest each time the intruder smashed something else.

A scream nearly released from her as he slammed whatever he carried on the top of the jewels above her head. The crunch of Styrofoam and papier-mâché made her heart stop. Thankfully she was deep enough in the chest that she didn't feel any real impact.

He cursed and screamed and Savannah remained still, praying for dawn. Even when he no longer made any noise and silence reigned, she remained where she was, afraid that he was still someplace in the lobby just waiting for her to show herself.

Time ticked by in agonizing seconds, in long, tormenting minutes. Savannah remained unmoving, afraid that even a deep breath might unsettle the "jewels" around her and give away her position.

Despite her fear, as time ticked by she must have

eventually fallen asleep, for the next voice she heard was Donnie's. "What in the hell happened in here? Savannah...Savannah, are you okay? Are you here?"

"I'm here," she replied, and as she dug herself out of the items around her, she saw the light of day drifting through the windows. She'd survived the horrible night, but the sight of daylight did nothing to ease the horror that still shot through her.

The tears she'd held in for what felt like a lifetime began to choke out of her as she fought her way to the top of the treasure chest and then climbed out and dropped to the floor.

Donnie ran to her, his wrinkled face and bushy salt-and-pepper eyebrows the most beautiful things she'd ever seen. He wrapped her in his arms. "Are you okay?" He looked around in shock. She followed his gaze and saw the damage that had been done in the darkness of the night.

"I'm sorry, Donnie," she cried. "I'm so sorry. Somebody got in here last night and tried to attack me. I'm so sorry about all the destruction."

"Hush," he said. "They're just things. They can easily be replaced. Are you sure you're okay?" He released his hold on her.

"No, I'm not okay," she replied with a barely suppressed sob. "I'm not okay at all. Please call Deputy Josh Griffin." She sank down to a sitting position with her back against the chest, shaking uncontrollably as she tried to process the night she'd just spent.

Donnie made the call to Josh, and Savannah remained where she was seated. At the moment all she wanted was Josh's arms around her. All she needed was the safety and security she knew she'd find there.

JOSH WAS JUST getting off duty when he got the call from Donnie telling him to get to the inn because something bad had happened overnight.

Donnie didn't waste time giving details, and Josh didn't waste time asking. All he knew was that Savannah had worked her shift last night, and the fact that anything bad had happened at the inn chilled his blood.

As he drove from his location toward the inn, he cursed himself for not asking questions. What exactly had happened? Was Savannah okay? Surely if she were seriously hurt Donnie would have called for an ambulance rather than calling him.

He stomped on the gas and wondered if he should call Trey or if Donnie had already done so. It didn't matter. If Trey hadn't been called, then Josh would assess the situation and decide whether the sheriff needed to be brought in.

He spun into the parking lot and saw only two vehicles, Savannah's navy sedan and Donnie's bright yellow pickup, indicating that there had probably been no overnight guests.

He parked and was out of the car in a shot. Donnie stood at the front door and opened it for him. The first thing that struck Josh was the utter devastation of the lobby. Pots were smashed, plants were overturned and even the coffee table in between the two sofas had a crack down the center.

The wooden chair behind the reception desk was in pieces, and his heart nearly stopped beating as he tried to process the destruction.

He took all this in in an instant. Then he saw Savannah seated by the huge gold treasure chest. The minute her gaze met his, she burst into tears, stumbled to her feet and raced into his arms.

"Are you all right?" he asked. He held her tight as she sobbed into the front of his shirt. What in the hell had happened in here? Who was responsible for all of this?

She nodded and continued to weep, her shoulders shaking and her body trembling against his. He kept his arms around her tightly, not asking any more questions and holding up a hand to stop Donnie from speaking.

It was obvious that at the moment, Savannah needed comfort, not questions. As he once again looked around at the damage, he tightened his arms around her, wishing he could take away the obvious trauma she'd suffered and pull it into himself.

She finally managed to gain some control and stepped away from him. She wiped her tears from her face but appeared unable to talk.

"I found this mess when I came in," Donnie said. "She was hiding in the treasure chest. She crawled out when I called her name. I was scared I'd find her dead somewhere."

It was the first time in all the years Josh had known

Donnie that the older man appeared shaken up. "Somebody made a mess in here. Thank God whoever it was didn't hurt Savannah."

"He wanted to kill me." Savannah finally found her voice. "I was at the desk, and it was about three fifteen or so and all the lights went out." She paused and visibly trembled.

Donnie walked over to one of the light switches and turned it on. Nothing happened. "The electricity is still off."

"At first I thought it was a blown fuse or something like that. I was just about to call Donnie when I heard the thumping of somebody walking the upstairs hallway."

"Old Peg Leg," Donnie said.

"It was no ghost," Savannah replied, her voice a little stronger now. "It was a living, breathing person, and he was definitely after me. He whispered my name and told me he was going to kill me."

A new chill worked through Josh. "He actually said your name?" he asked.

She nodded and wrapped her arms around herself as she began to tremble once again. Josh pulled out his cell phone and called Trey. This was definitely something the sheriff needed to know about.

With the call completed, he dropped his phone back into his pocket, placed an arm around Savannah's shoulder and led her to one of the two sofas.

He pulled her down next to him as Donnie disappeared into a back room and returned a few minutes later with a broom. "Donnie, you shouldn't do any cleanup yet. I'm sure the sheriff will want some of his men to process this as a crime scene," Josh said.

Donnie leaned the broom against a wall and sat on the sofa opposite them. "I can't figure out how anyone got inside. The front door was locked when I got here, and so was the back door. The only door that wasn't locked was the one in my office that leads down to the basement. And there are no windows to break into down there."

That didn't mean there wasn't another way into the inn. Josh thought of the tunnel system and wondered if there was some way into the basement that Donnie wasn't aware of.

He'd check it out once Trey arrived. "I'm not going to ask you questions now," he told Savannah. "Trey will want to question you, and there's no need for you to go through the details twice."

"I'll just say I've never been so grateful to hear Donnie's voice," she replied and looked at her boss fondly.

"After walking in and seeing the mess, I was just glad to see you alive and well," Donnie said gruffly.

The attacker had called her by name, Josh thought. There was no denying that whoever had been in here last night had been here specifically to hurt or kill Savannah.

Josh had thought the attack in the tunnel might have just been an accident of strange circumstances, but this changed everything. This attack had been personal, and she was the intended target.

It didn't take long for Trey and his favorite deputy, Ray McClure, to arrive, along with Deputy Daniel Carson, who said he'd heard the official dispatch and had decided to stop in at the end of his shift.

Josh was grateful to see his friend, who he knew was a better investigator than Trey and Ray put together.

"Jeez, it looks like a bomb exploded in here," Ray exclaimed. He walked around, shards of broken pottery crunching beneath his feet.

"Stand still," Trey said irritably to Ray as he sat next to Savannah on the sofa. "Let's hear what happened, and then we'll proceed from there."

Savannah recounted the night from the moment she arrived to when she went into the restroom and then returned to her desk and the lights went out.

As she spoke about the thumping noise and then the whisper of her name as the person came down the stairs, Josh wanted to wrap her in his arms once again and carry her far away from here.

She explained that she had hidden behind a plant pot and listened while the intruder had raged, smashing things and promising to kill her when he found her.

"And you didn't recognize his voice?" Trey asked.

"I felt like I should know it, but no, I couldn't identify it. It was gruff, like he was trying to disguise it," she said. She went on to talk about the flashlight he clicked on. She had known her hiding place behind a plant wouldn't keep her safe. That was when she decided to climb into the treasure chest and bury herself deep inside.

"Did you see him at all?" Trey asked in a concerned tone.

She shook her head. "He was just a dark shadow, and I think he was wearing a ski mask." She looked at Donnie and gave him a tense smile. "I've joked about that treasure chest being a monstrosity forever, but last night it definitely saved my life."

"It is a monstrosity, but I figure once the amusement park opens, tourists will want their pictures taken in front of it," Donnie replied.

"Unfortunately, if you want to try to pull fingerprints, I'm not sure he touched anything except with whatever bat or wooden stake he used to smash everything," she said to Trey.

"If he touched anything upstairs or the stairway itself, you should be able to pull some prints. I had Dorothy dust everything yesterday," Donnie added.

"Ray and Daniel, why don't you start in the guest rooms and see what prints you can pull off furniture or door frames?" Trey instructed. "I'll call in Deputies Bream and Stiller to help."

Trey got up from the sofa and took several steps away to make his calls. Donnie also got up and stood next to the treasure chest, surveying the surroundings.

Josh scooted closer to Savannah, his heart filled with the terror she must have felt through the long ordeal. "Thank God you were able to hide," he said softly.

"I don't understand why this happened," she said,

and he was grateful to see that her trembling had finally stopped, although her eyes still retained a depth of darkness that he knew was trauma.

"Let's talk about that," Trey said as he resumed his seat next to her. "You said you can't imagine why this happened? Can you think of anyone who might have a reason to want you dead?"

"No. I don't have anything to do with anyone. I haven't had any interaction, good or bad, with anyone for a long time. The only person I see on a regular basis is Chad Wilson, who delivers my groceries to me once a week."

"Has he ever had any issue with you?" Trey asked.

"No, although last time he came by, he asked me out and I turned him down, but he seemed to understand that the problem wasn't him, that I just didn't date at all. He stayed and visited for a while after that, so I thought everything was fine. I can't imagine Chad doing something like this."

Trey wrote for a moment in a small notepad he'd pulled from his pocket and then looked back at her. "We'll check Chad's whereabouts last night."

Deputy Derrick Bream and Deputy Wes Stiller arrived with their fingerprinting kits and were sent upstairs to join the other two deputies.

"What about Bo McBride? Have you had any interaction with him since he's been back in town?" Trey asked.

"No, but why would Bo want to hurt me?" she asked with a frown.

"Maybe he thinks you know something about your sister's death that could put him behind bars," Trey replied.

"So he's waited two years to attack me?" Savannah scoffed. "You know I don't believe Bo killed Shelly, and I'm sure he's not behind any plan to kill me now."

"I think a good question is how the perp got into the building," Josh said, knowing Bo McBride and the murder of Shelly was a touchy subject with Savannah. "According to Donnie, all of the outside doors were locked when he arrived this morning."

"You think a tunnel?" Trey asked.

"I think it's not only possible but probable," Josh replied.

"But Savannah said he came from upstairs," Trey said.

"And she was also in the restroom right before things went down. It's possible he came up from the basement and went upstairs while she was in the bathroom."

"Then how did he turn out the lights from upstairs?" Savannah asked.

"We'll figure out the answers, but right now I'd like to get a look in the basement," Trey said.

"I'm coming with you," Josh replied.

"And so am I." Savannah stood, a resolute expression on her face.

"Donnie," Trey called to the man who had remained standing next to the treasure chest. "Is there something strange in your basement?"

Donnie frowned. "I've got lots of what most people would consider strange down in the basement. I'm not sure what you're talking about."

"We need to go down there and check things out," Trey said.

Donnie shrugged. "Fine with me." He led them through the lobby to his private office, a small room with a desk, a computer and paperwork stacked on several file cabinets. He opened a door and turned on a light that illuminated a set of stairs leading down.

"I'm not sure what you're looking for, but feel free to snoop around," he said.

Trey led the way, with Savannah behind him and Josh following. The stairs were narrow, and once they reached the bottom, it was obvious Donnie had more than a few hoarding tendencies.

"I hope we don't have to move all these boxes and crap to find a tunnel in the floor," Trey said.

"If there is a tunnel and that's how the perp got in, then he wouldn't have had a way to stack anything back on top of the entrance once he left," Josh said. "We're going to find a place either in the wall or on the floor that's bare."

They fell silent as they searched. Josh was positive that there was a tunnel entrance somewhere that had allowed the perp to sneak in.

The fuse box showed nothing to indicate that the fuses had been blown, so the perp had obviously ma-nipulated the electricity another way. They would have to call somebody from the electric company to find the issue and fix it.

The walls were made of concrete blocks, and it was Savannah who found the first loose one. She called the men over, and by the time five blocks had been removed, a tunnel entrance was revealed.

"So now we know how he got inside," Trey said. He pulled a flashlight from his belt and shone it down into the tunnel. "I'll have to get some equipment before I go in."

Josh nodded. He understood the reluctance of anyone to go into an unknown tunnel without the proper items to mark an exit out.

"If you've gotten all you need from Savannah, I'm going to follow her home," Josh said.

"Yeah, if I need to ask any more questions I know where she lives," Trey said absently, his light still focused into the darkness beyond the blocks.

"Oh, and if you don't mind, I'm officially taking vacation time as of right now," Josh said. "I have plenty of time coming to me."

Trey straightened up and looked at Savannah and then at Josh. "Are you planning on pulling some sort of private bodyguard duty?"

"Something like that," Josh replied. He touched Savannah's elbow. "I'd say your night here has been long enough. Let's head out."

He followed her up the stairs, his thoughts racing. When they reached the lobby, once again he was struck by the rage that had been unleashed…a killing rage.

The fact that it had been directed at Savannah chilled him to his very soul. There was only one way he knew to keep her safe, and that was why he intended to take charge of things whether she liked it or not.

"Donnie, Savannah is officially on an undetermined leave of absence as of right now," he said to the owner. Savannah looked at him in surprise but didn't argue with him.

Donnie nodded as if he'd expected it. "I'll call in some of my other gals to take up the slack. Besides, it's going to take me a couple of days to get things cleaned up."

"I hope you have insurance," Savannah said.

Donnie smiled gently at her. "Those pots were cheap enough, and I've probably got extra ones in the basement somewhere. I won't be making an insurance claim. A little elbow grease and things will be good as new. You just stay safe, Savannah."

"She will. I'm going to see to it," Josh replied. He turned to look at her. "I'll follow you home."

She nodded. "I just need to get my purse from the drawer in the desk." She retrieved her purse, and then together they left the inn.

The sun was up, and it was almost ten. Josh followed her car as they drove to her house. She had to be not only exhausted but also still experiencing some kind of posttraumatic stress from the horrifying night she'd just survived.

Making sure she got home safely from the inn was just the first part of his plan to assure her safety. She probably wasn't going to like the next stage of his plan, but he couldn't get past the knowledge that whoever had been in the inn last night had been filled with rage, and he'd named Savannah as his victim.

Josh had let down Savannah years ago when it came to pushing for an intensive, clean investigation into Shelly's death. He wasn't about to let her down now.

Chapter Eight

Savannah found herself alternately flashing with warmth and shivering with chills as she drove home. She tried not to replay the events of the night anymore in her mind.

It was over. The sun was up and she'd survived the long, terrifying night. As she glanced in her rearview mirror, the sight of Josh's car just behind hers reassured her. All she had to do was get home and lock the windows and doors and she'd be fine. Maybe she'd get a security system installed, and then she'd never leave her house again.

She had enough money saved up that would see her through a couple of months jobless, and surely by then Trey and his men would be able to figure out who was after her and why.

She tightened her fingers on the steering wheel. Who had been in the inn last night? Who wanted her dead? Whoever it was had been so violently angry. No matter how long she thought about it, she couldn't come up with an answer.

Punching the button that would open her garage door, she tried to shove away any thoughts of the night, tried to reach the same level of numbness that had been such a constant friend of hers since Shelly's death.

She drove into the garage and got out of her car and then walked back to where Josh had parked in the driveway. "Get in," he said.

She frowned in confusion. "Why?"

"Because we're going to my place. I'm going to pack a bag, and you're going to have a houseguest until we get all this sorted out. So, get in."

Her initial reaction was to protest, but her lingering fear was greater than her pride or her desire to be alone. She got into his car.

"I expected an argument," he said as he backed out of her driveway.

"To be honest, I'm scared. I'll let you stay with me until I can get a security system installed. Then I'll be fine alone."

He cast her a doubtful glance. "Do you have any idea how easy it is to get around a security system if you know what you're doing?"

"Don't tell me," she replied. The idea of a houseguest wasn't particularly pleasant. The idea of Josh as a houseguest was even less desirable. He bothered her in ways she didn't like with just short contact with him. The idea of him living in her house felt very wrong.

But the idea of him being with her day and night also made her feel safe, and right now she needed that more than anything else. She didn't even want to acknowledge that a hint of excitement also filled her as she thought of spending time with him.

She could put her discomfort at sharing her space aside for a feeling of safety. She needed sleep after the long night, and she had a feeling that without Josh nearby, and knowing there was a tunnel entrance right in her own backyard, she'd never really sleep again.

They arrived at Josh's house, and he followed her to the front door. He unlocked it and they stepped inside. "Just hang tight. It shouldn't take me long." He disappeared down the hallway to the master bedroom.

Savannah knew that the tight control she'd had on her life had flown away. Things were happening spontaneously, without her control, and that was more than a little frightening in and of itself.

True to his word, Josh took only a few minutes and then reappeared with a large duffel bag in hand. Savannah frowned. "That looks like enough clothes to stay a long time."

"I intend to stay until the danger is over. Savannah, I know this isn't the way you want to live your life. I know the last thing you want is anyone staying in your house. But you have to face the fact that somebody wants you dead and this isn't the time for you to be alone."

"I know." She released a deep sigh. "Let's just get back to my place and you can get settled in."

"And hopefully you can get some sleep." They stepped back outside.

"I imagine you could use some of that yourself. You've been up working all night, too."

"I'll catch some snooze time. Don't worry about me."

Within minutes they were back at her house. She led him to Mac's old bedroom, the first one in the hallway. Josh set his duffel bag on the bed. "And you have the master suite?" he asked.

"No, I'm in the bedroom next door. The master suite has been empty since Mom and Dad moved away. I've stayed in the room I shared with Shelly since childhood."

"I need to see it," he said. "In fact, I need to see all the rooms."

She knew it wasn't mere curiosity but rather a need to check out windows and such for security purposes. She started the tour in the master suite, which held nothing but some storage boxes she'd gone through after her parents had left.

"Do you ever use this room for anything?" he asked. He was all business, his gaze sharp as he looked into the master bath and then returned to where she stood.

"No, not really. I use the bathroom in here, but I can always use the one in the hallway."

"Then I think the first thing we'll do is buy a doorknob with a lock so that nobody can come in through the windows and through the door into the main living area."

His words made her realize just how seriously he was taking her safety. They left the master suite, and she showed him a small bedroom across from hers. It was a guest room with just a double bed and a dresser.

"We'll do the same thing to this room," he said after checking to make sure the window was locked. "It's not used, and so we'll make access into the house a little more difficult."

A wave of shyness swept over Savannah as she led him into her room with its double bed, dresser and minishrine to Shelly on top of the desk.

He checked the window first to make sure it was locked and then paused by the desk, looking at the items. "A ceramic frog? There has to be a story behind that."

A bittersweet smile curved her lips. "Bo gave that to Shelly when he proposed to her. The ring was in the frog's mouth, and he told her she'd never kiss a frog because she'd spend the rest of her life kissing him."

Josh frowned. "We never found her engagement ring."

"You never found her real killer," she replied and immediately wanted to call the words back. "I'm sorry. I really don't want to talk about that now. All I want is to take a shower and fall into bed." At least the hallway bathroom was windowless, so she didn't have to worry about anyone coming inside.

"While you shower I'll get my things unpacked," Josh replied. "And we need to keep your bedroom door open at all times so that I can hear if you might be in trouble."

"Okay," she agreed. She didn't particularly like it,

but she'd like it even less if somebody managed to get through her window and attempted to get to her. She wanted Josh to be able to hear everything, even if she snored.

She grabbed a clean nightgown from a drawer and headed for the bathroom. It was only when she stood beneath the hot spray of the shower that she began to weep as the trauma of the night gripped her once again.

Leaning weakly against the shower stall, she wept with fear not only for what she had experienced but also for what the future held. If somebody wanted her dead and that person wasn't identified, he would probably eventually succeed.

There was only so much Josh could do to keep her safe. He could stay here, but it would take only a single shot through the kitchen window, a sniper's bullet, to find her while she had her morning coffee.

Somebody had wanted her sister dead and had succeeded. Why should Savannah be any different? She just hoped that before she died, she'd know who was responsible and why they had wanted her dead.

JOSH PLACED HIS gun on the coffee table, stretched out on the sofa and closed his eyes. Savannah had showered and was now sleeping soundly in bed. He hadn't wanted to go to Mac's room and crawl into bed, for he feared his sleep would be too deep.

He figured he'd sleep lightly on the sofa and awaken easily at any alien noise that might mean danger, although he was expecting a quiet afternoon. The attacker had been up all night and had expended a lot of energy. Even the bad guys had to rest sometime.

Josh needed to catch some shut-eye, but his brain raced, making it impossible for sleep to break through the chaos. Who had been in that inn last night, and who on earth would want to kill Savannah?

She'd lived like a virtual recluse for the last two years, so the odds seemed slim that she'd done something to somebody that would warrant this kind of reaction.

Could the attack be related to Shelly's death? He just couldn't believe that a murder that had taken place two years before had anything to do with the threat to Savannah now. Had Chad Wilson taken her rejection of him more seriously than she'd thought? Was Eric Baptiste involved?

He finally drifted off to sleep and was shocked to realize it was nearing dusk when he awakened. The first thing he did was jump up off the sofa and check on Savannah, who was still sound asleep.

He checked the rest of the house and then went into the kitchen and raided the cabinets until he found the coffee and cups and then put on a pot to brew and sat at the kitchen table.

He pulled out his cell phone and dialed Daniel, assuming he'd probably be up and around by now after his night shift and work at the inn that morning.

"Did I wake you?" he asked when Daniel answered.

"Nah, I was just getting ready to make me a sandwich."

"How did things go after we left this morning?"

"No fingerprints found, no sign of forced entry, so we are sure the perp came in through the tunnel."

"Did you all check out the tunnel?" Josh asked. He got up to pour himself a cup of coffee.

"Trey called Mayor Burns, and the two of them and Ray went in, but I haven't heard what they found. Trey sent me home to get some sleep. You might check with him. How is Savannah doing?"

"She's still asleep. I've moved into her place for the time being. I swear, Daniel, I can't figure out who might have a beef with her."

"I don't know. It all started with that attack in the tunnel," Daniel said. "And the only person we've learned about so far who knew about the tunnel system is Eric Baptiste."

"Who supposedly had become friends with Shelly just before her murder." Josh heaved a sigh of frustration.

"If Eric knows anything about Shelly's murder, he's not talking," Daniel said.

"I still can't figure out a connection between Shelly's murder and what's happening now. It's been two years. Maybe since Eric knew about the tunnel network, it's possible that somebody else knows and thinks Savannah is a threat to whatever is going on down there."

"We've got to figure out if something is going on in the tunnels, something worth killing for," Daniel replied.

"Eat your sandwich. You've given me plenty of food

for thought," Josh said. The two men disconnected, and Josh carried his coffee cup back to the table and sat.

He called Trey to get an update and was still seated at the table thirty minutes later when Savannah entered the kitchen. Her hair was sleep-tousled, and a pink robe wrapped around her and was belted at her slender waist.

"Sleep well?" he asked and tried not to notice how sexy she looked with her sleepy eyes and bedhead.

"Like a log," she replied. "What about you? Did you get in some shut-eye?" She walked across the room to the coffeepot.

"I just woke up about an hour ago," he replied. "I think it would be a good thing if we could work into twisting our hours to normal ones so we sleep at night and are awake during the day."

She joined him at the table and wrapped her hands around her coffee mug. "Why?"

"Because I think we need to spend our days out and about and doing a little investigating of our own."

Her eyes widened as if he'd just asked her to walk a tightrope between two skyscrapers. "I really don't like the idea of being out and about."

"I know I'm asking you to leave your comfort zone, but to be honest, I think Trey is more interested in investigating the tunnels than he is in investigating who might be after you. I just think we need to be proactive."

She took a sip of the coffee, her eyes dark and

fathomless over the rim of her cup as she stared at him. "Proactive, how?"

"We need to talk to Bo, and I want to check out this Chad guy who delivers your groceries every week. You should be seen in town, and we can gauge people's reactions to you."

She lowered her cup slowly and stared past his shoulder and out the window, where the last gasp of twilight painted the scenery in deep purple shades. "You have no idea what you're asking of me." She looked back at him.

"I think I do," he countered. "You've hidden out here for two years, and I'm asking you to leave your safe haven because I don't think it's necessarily safe anymore." He was asking her to rejoin life again, and he hoped in doing so he wasn't putting her more at risk of death.

"I'm safe with you here," she protested.

"I don't want us to be sitting ducks here. I want to find out who is behind the attacks on you, and we can't do that just by hanging out here."

"Okay. We'll do it your way," she said, but he could tell the idea didn't sit well with her. "In the meantime, I don't know about you, but I'm starving."

She jumped up from the table and went to the refrigerator. "How about cheese and mushroom omelets with toast? Usually when I wake up at this time of night, I'm ready for breakfast food."

"Sounds good to me," he agreed. He had a feeling

her sudden starvation came from her need to change the subject. "What can I do to help?" he asked.

"Just sit there and stay out of my way," she replied.

He figured what she'd really like to do is pretend he wasn't there. But he was here, and he wasn't going anywhere until the danger to her had been neutralized.

She worked silently, cutting up mushrooms and whisking eggs in a mixing bowl. He watched her, enjoying the sight of her as she bustled around, a look of fierce concentration on her face.

She deserved so much better than what she'd given herself over the last two years. She should be having lunch out with girlfriends, enjoying drinks and dinner at Jimmy's Place.

It was ironic that he was pulling her back into life because somebody wanted her dead. The truth was, he remembered the rush to judgment in Shelly's murder, and he didn't trust Trey to investigate the attempts on Savannah's life adequately.

When Josh had spoken to Trey on the phone earlier, Trey had even implied that perhaps Savannah had done all the damage to the inn herself the night before, that she was seeking new attention since she was no longer doing her ghost walks. Josh had only just managed to tamp down his outrage at his boss.

"I spoke to Trey just before you woke up," he now said.

Savannah poured the egg mixture into an awaiting omelet pan and then looked at him expectantly. "Did they find anything? Fingerprints or any useful evidence?"

"No, nothing like that. Mayor Burns showed up, and he and Trey and Ray went into the tunnel and followed it until they reached a three-pronged fork. They remained in the main tunnel and found an exit at the edge of the swamp shanties but didn't get a chance to complete their exploration of the other two forks. They plan to do that tomorrow."

She placed four slices of bread in the toaster and pressed down on the knob. "So, it's possible that whoever came out into the inn came from that entrance near the swamp. Both Eric and Chad would know that area."

"Chad is from the swamp side of town?" Josh asked. "I don't think I've ever met him."

She nodded and flipped the omelet pan to the other side. "He's four or five years younger than us. He's Sharon's son and mostly works in the back of Sharon's grocery store, so you probably haven't seen him there. Sharon lived in one of the shanties when Chad was growing up. He told me he was fifteen when his mother finally moved them to a house near the store. He doesn't strike me as the type who would get into trouble."

"That's what we thought about Coach Cantor, and he wound up being a sick stalker bent on killing Claire Silver," Josh reminded her. "Just because he's nice when he delivers your groceries doesn't mean he shouldn't be looked at more closely."

"All I know is that I want whoever is after me behind bars sooner rather than later." She moved the pan off the burner and turned toward the counter as the toast popped up.

It wasn't long before they were seated at the table and eating. The silence between them grew to an uncomfortable level as Josh tried to think of a topic that might be neutral and pleasant.

She didn't appear bothered by the silence, but then she probably wouldn't be. He imagined she was accustomed to it. But he found it odd to sit at a table with another person and not have any conversation at all.

"What do you do when you're here in the house all day?" he finally asked.

She looked up from her plate and frowned thoughtfully. "I spend a lot of the day sleeping, and then when I'm up, I watch television or clean house. Sometimes I work on creating new recipes or read. What do you do during your spare time?"

"Like you, I sleep during part of the day, and then I sometimes meet Daniel for a late lunch or I hang out at Jimmy's Place and socialize."

"I still think of Jimmy's Place as Bo's Place," she replied. "I haven't been in there since Bo sold it to Jimmy and left town."

"Maybe we'll have a late lunch there tomorrow."

"Why would we do that? I can make lunch here," she protested.

"Because I've often seen Bo and Claire there in the afternoons, and talking to them is as good a place as any to start our own investigation."

"I can't imagine that they'd have any information that might tell us who is after me," she replied.

"They've been stirring up things about Shelly's murder. Who knows what they might know or what other gossip we might hear while there that will move us forward."

She shook her head. "I hate this. I hate all of it. I was perfectly content with living life on my terms, and now I feel like I'm being forced out of my comfort zone."

"Taking steps out of your comfort zone isn't always a bad thing," he countered softly.

She looked at him dubiously. "And when was the last time you stepped out of your comfort zone?"

"The night I had you over for dinner," he replied easily. "You were the first woman I've ever invited to dinner at my house. I can't remember the last time I was so nervous, except when I heard there'd been trouble at the inn."

"You were nervous to have me to dinner?" A tiny smile danced at the corner of her lips.

"Terrified," he replied. "I wanted the night to go perfectly, and I was afraid I'd accidentally stick a fork in my eye or catch my pants on fire while I was grilling the steaks."

She giggled. "You're silly."

"Maybe you need a little silly in your life right now," he replied.

Her giggle instantly died. "Josh, don't push me. The fact that you're here in my house, the idea of going out and mingling with other people and the knowledge that somebody wants to kill me are more than enough for me to handle right now."

"I just remember the young woman who used to flirt with me, the one who laughed so easily and made me want to be around her," he said.

Her eyes darkened once again. "That woman is gone and she's never coming back."

"You have no idea how much I mourn her passing," he said with more emotion than he'd intended.

Her cheeks flushed with a faint pink tone, and she glanced away from him. She started to rise from the table and then sat once again, her eyes huge. "Josh, I just saw somebody at the window."

Chapter Nine

Adrenaline flushed through him. "Act normal," he instructed her. "Clear the table and pretend that nothing is wrong. Don't look toward the window again. I'm going to grab my gun and go out the front door. I'll lock it behind me. Don't open it again for anyone except me."

He got up from the table and sauntered out of the room with a forced ease. The minute he left the kitchen, he raced for his gun and was out the front door.

The hot July night smacked him in the face but didn't slow him down. He ran to one side of the house and peeked around the corner. Seeing nobody there, he ran to the next corner that would show him the backyard.

Thankfully the moon was three-quarters full, spilling down enough illumination for him to see without any artificial light. He gazed around the corner and saw a figure clad in black moving across the yard.

"Halt," Josh cried and then cursed as the person took off running. He wasn't about to shoot an unknown person in the back for window peeping. "Stop or I'll shoot," he bluffed.

Apparently, the man knew it was a bluff because he didn't slow down. With another curse Josh took off after him. Whoever it was appeared physically fit, and Josh had to push himself in order to make any gain on him.

The window peeper ran across the backyards of several houses and jumped a chain link fence, which started a dog barking frantically. Josh reached the fence as the perp flew over the opposite side of the fence and cut between two houses, disappearing from Josh's view.

Instead of jumping the fence, Josh raced along the edge of it to the front of the house, but the perp had disappeared. Josh crept as silently as possible, his gun still in his hand as he passed the house with the fence, and spun around the corner to see if the "Peeping Tom" might be hunkered down there.

Nobody was there. There wasn't even a shed or out-building for him to have hidden in. Josh looked across the street, where there was also no sign of the person.

He had no idea where to go next. The hunt was over and the man had gotten away. He turned to head back to Savannah's house. Dammit, if he'd just been a little faster he might have caught the man and solved the mystery of the attacks on Savannah.

There was no way he really believed that some teenager or creep was trying to get a cheap thrill by peeking into a window. This felt far more ominous, considering what Savannah had been through the night before.

Josh's car was in the driveway, so whoever it was had to know that she wasn't alone in the house.

Had he just looked in to make sure Josh was really there? Was he trying to get an idea of the floor plan of the home? Or was he obsessed enough that he'd just needed to catch a glimpse of Savannah?

It was the last possibility that worried him. Who could be obsessed with a woman who had been nothing more than a ghost in the past two years? And why would that obsession be fed by a killing rage against her?

A new thought struck him, one that had him racing back to Savannah's house as quickly as physically possible. Had the person in the backyard simply been a ruse to get him out of the house, leaving Savannah alone with the real threat?

His heart pounded with new anxiety. He reached Savannah's front door and knocked a frantic rhythm. "Savannah, it's me."

She opened the door to allow him inside, and he breathed a sigh of relief. "I'm assuming you didn't catch him," she said as they walked back to the kitchen.

"He had too much of a head start, and then I lost him." Josh placed his gun on the table and flopped down in a chair at the table, still slightly winded by his unsuccessful race.

"You think it was my attacker?" she asked and sat across from him, worry evident on her features.

"I think we'd be foolish to believe it wasn't," he replied.

"He told me I screwed things up," she said more to herself than to him.

Josh sat up straighter in his chair. "You didn't mention that before."

"I just remembered it. He said he was going to kill me because I screwed everything up." She gazed at him in confusion. "How could I possibly have screwed up anything for anyone?"

"You said Chad Wilson asked you out and you turned him down. Maybe you screwed things up for him because you didn't indicate any romantic interest in him. Or maybe Eric Baptiste is using the tunnels for something other than finding plants and roots for his mother's shop."

Josh got up and poured himself a cup of the coffee and returned to the table. "Daniel reminded me that the first attack on you took place in the tunnel, and after that, the tunnel network was no longer a secret."

"I ruined things because it's my fault the tunnel network was no longer a secret?"

"It's a theory, but not the only one," he replied. "It's possible this has nothing to do with the tunnels, and it's also possible it has everything to do with the tunnels."

"Jeez, thanks for making me feel better," she replied drily.

"I just don't want us to have tunnel vision, no pun intended," he replied. When he was involved in the investigation into Shelly's death, Trey had suffered from tunnel vision, focusing on one suspect to the exclusion of any others. Josh wasn't going to let that happen again. "I should probably call Trey and tell him about this latest event."

"Why? What's the point of bothering him? I'm assuming you couldn't identify the person at the window. I only got a quick glance at him, and he was wearing a ski mask."

"You're right," Josh replied in frustration. "I just wish I had caught him. Then we might have all the answers we need. Case closed."

She glanced toward the window and then looked back at him. "Why don't we go into the living room? I feel like I'm on stage sitting here in front of these windows."

He took a last sip of his coffee and then placed the cup in the dishwasher. He followed her into the living room, where she sat on one side of the sofa and he sat on the opposite and placed his gun on the coffee table in easy reach.

"I still don't understand why I was attacked in the tunnel," she said. "And you already knew about them when I was attacked."

"Yeah, but nobody else knew that I knew about them," he reminded her. He grimaced. "If I'd told somebody instead of agreeing to let you make that final walk, then you wouldn't have been attacked."

"If Shelly hadn't gone alone to the stone bench down by the lagoon the night that she did, then she wouldn't have been murdered," she countered. "We can't go back and change things."

"I know, but I wish I could," he replied.

She looked at him curiously. "What would you change?"

He leaned back against the sofa cushion. "I would

have insisted Jacob not get into a car with a bunch of his friends and a driver I knew liked to speed and drive recklessly. I would have fought to get Trey to do a more thorough investigation into your sister's death, and I definitely would have asked you out over two years ago instead of being afraid you'd turn me down."

She gazed at him in surprise. "You were afraid I'd turn you down?" He nodded. A wistful smile curved her lips. "And at that time, I was afraid you'd never ask me out. Then Shelly was murdered and everything changed, and now there's no going back."

There was such finality to her words. While he believed she was still attracted to him and he certainly was still attracted to her, she intimated that there was no chance for them to ever act on that attraction.

He was here not because she wanted him here but because she needed his protection. She'd made it clear that she had no desire to change the isolation she'd crawled into in this house.

He might be able to change things for an investigation. He could force her out of the house, make her interact with other people, but ultimately he had a feeling that once she was no longer in danger, she would return to the isolation that seemed to bring her comfort but no happiness.

Savannah awakened at ten the next morning, dreading the day to come. She and Josh had stayed up until three and then had agreed to head to bed and get up earlier than usual for both of them this morning to start their foray into the public arena of Lost Lagoon.

She didn't want to go out. She didn't want to talk to other people, but she did want answers, and if Josh thought they might find some by going out, then she'd just suck it up and go along with his plan.

Hopefully this would all resolve itself quickly. She glanced toward the desk that held Shelly's memorabilia. She knew it was grief that drove her to remain disconnected from anything and everyone. But the grief had become familiar. It felt so safe and comfortable.

She dragged herself out of bed and pulled on her robe. Though filled with dread, she moved her feet down the hallway toward the bathroom. The scent of coffee let her know that Josh was already up.

She opened the bathroom door and gasped. Josh stood at the sink clad only in a white towel wrapped around his slim hips. Half of his face was covered in shaving cream, and his eyes widened in the mirror at the sight of her.

"Oh, sorry," she exclaimed and told her feet to move backward and out the door. Her feet weren't listening. In fact, she was brain-dead. The only thing working in her head was the visual feast of his broad, muscled chest, his lean waist, his slim hips and the length of his athletic legs.

Heat rushed through her, the heat of fierce desire. He was gorgeous with his clothes on, but with just a towel around his waist, he was sex with shaving cream.

"Uh…do you want to help me finish shaving?" he asked with a touch of amusement.

His voice snapped her brain back into control. She grabbed the doorknob, stumbled backward and slammed the door closed.

She went back into her bedroom and sat on the edge of the bed, trying to erase the vision of Josh from her mind. It was impossible. It was stuck in her brain like Spanish moss in a cypress tree.

As if the day wasn't going to be difficult enough, she thought. Now she had to deal with the vision of a very hot, very sexy man in her head.

It was eleven when they left the house. Thankfully neither of them had mentioned that moment in the bathroom. He'd been fully dressed when he'd peeked into her bedroom and told her the bathroom was all hers.

She couldn't remember the last time she'd been outside the house during the day. She had dressed in a pair of white capris, a gold-tone sleeveless top and sandals, and as Josh backed out of the driveway her nerves roared to life.

Josh was dressed casually in a pair of jeans with a navy-blue T-shirt tucked in. Around his waist he wore his gun and holster, letting her know that while he chatted about driving around town and stopping in at Jimmy's Place for lunch, he hadn't forgotten their real purpose and his self-proclaimed duty to keep her safe.

"It's a beautiful day," he said as they left her neighborhood and headed for Main Street.

"It's hot and sticky," she replied.

He pointed up to the ridge where the construction of the new amusement park was happening. "It looks like they're making good progress."

"It's just going to ruin the town with all the commercialism."

He shot her an amused glance. "Do you intend to be perverse all day?"

"Maybe. I haven't decided yet." She shot him a small smile. "Actually I'm not trying to be perverse. I'm just nervous," she admitted.

"You don't have to be nervous. As long as I'm by your side, I swear nothing bad is going to happen to you."

"I know that," she replied and turned her head to look out the passenger window. What he didn't understand was that a threat to her physical being was only part of her anxiety.

She had been pleasantly numb for almost two years, caring about nobody and fine with the fact that nobody cared about her. She was afraid that somehow this entire experience was going to make her care again, feel again.

They passed the Pirate's Inn, and she fought against a shiver as she remembered the night of terror she'd spent there. She wondered if she'd ever be able to go back to work there when this was all over.

"Where are we going first?" she asked.

"Hardware store to get locks for the spare room and master suite," he replied. "And after that, since it's still early, I thought we'd stop by Claire Silver's place and talk to her and Bo. Maybe their unofficial investigation into Shelly's death has stirred up something that has to do with what's happening to you now."

"I just can't imagine the two things being tied together," she replied.

"To be honest, neither can I, but I intend to leave no stone unturned. If nothing else, we can exclude that possibility and move on to the next."

"Do you have a definite next?" she asked.

He cast her a quick grin. "I'm working on it as we speak."

She looked out the passenger window again as a vision of Josh in that darned towel flashed in her head. Even now she could smell the lingering scent of shaving lotion coupled with minty soap and the spice of his cologne.

She was grateful to get out of the car when they arrived at the hardware store. It took only minutes to buy the locks and then return to the car that smelled of him. When he pulled up in front of Claire Silver's house, Savannah was grateful to get away from his evocative scent.

Claire lived on the shanty side of town. The swamp came precariously close to the backyards of the row of shanties that lined this particular street.

Some of the shanty-like structures were little more than abandoned lean-tos that had once served as homes to poverty-stricken families. Others, like Claire's, had been renovated into cute, neat homes.

"Mayor Burns is probably going to have all the

abandoned shanties pulled down before the amusement park opens," Josh said as he parked in front of Claire's place. "He'll consider them a blight on the town and a detriment to the tourist trade."

"Those shanties were the first structures to make the town. It's kind of sad to tear down the history just because it isn't pretty," she said.

They got out of the car and walked toward Claire's front door. Savannah steeled herself for talking to Bo for the first time in two years. He'd dated Shelly since high school and for ten years after that. He had been the big brother to Savannah that Mac had never been.

She'd also been friendly with Claire and now considered her a good partner for Bo. She had no resentment that Bo had moved on. She wanted only happiness for him.

Josh knocked and Bo opened the door. He looked at her and flew out the door and pulled her into a hug. "Sweet Savannah," he whispered in her ear.

He smelled just like he had when he'd been dating Shelly, like clean male and a faint woodsy cologne. She hugged him back and fought back tears. He finally released her and stepped back. "I can't tell you how much I've wanted to contact you since I've been back in town. Come on, let's go inside where it's cool."

Claire stood from the sofa as they all came inside. Greetings were exchanged all around, and they landed at Claire's kitchen table to talk.

"We heard about what happened at the inn," Claire said. "I'm so glad you're okay."

"I plan to keep her okay despite the fact that somebody wants her dead," Josh said.

Claire's blue eyes darkened, and she reached across the table and captured Savannah's hand in hers. "I know exactly what you're going through. I know the fear of not knowing who you can trust." She released Savannah's hand and narrowed her gaze at Josh. "Don't tell me you're here because you think Bo had anything to do with the attack on Savannah."

"Quite the contrary. We're here to see if, during your investigation into what happened two years ago, you might have stumbled on something that put Savannah at risk," Josh replied.

Bo frowned. "Nothing that I can think of, but we haven't managed to dig up much of anything new about that night. Our investigation got sidetracked when Roger Cantor, the high school coach who turned into an obsessed stalker, came after Claire."

"Did you know that before her death, Shelly had become friends with Eric Baptiste?" Josh asked.

Bo nodded. "Yeah, I knew about their friendship." He looked at Savannah, his gaze soft with caring. "You and I both know that Shelly probably wasn't ever going to marry me. As much as we loved each other, she wanted out of this town. I wondered if she saw Eric as her ticket out of town."

"How so?" Savannah asked.

"I know Eric has a degree. He could probably go anywhere in the country and get a job teaching. Maybe she thought she could talk him into leaving Lost Lagoon and taking her with him," Bo said.

"Do you think he's the person who met Shelly that night? Do you think he murdered her?" Savannah asked, a jumble of emotions rushing through her.

"I don't know," Bo said. Once again his gaze went to Josh. "All I know for sure is that I didn't kill Shelly."

"And you have no clue who might be after Savannah," Josh asked.

"None, but I want you to see to it that she stays safe." Once again Bo looked at her, and in his eyes she saw the caring, the tenderness that spoke of old days and bittersweet memories.

It was too much for her. Those memories of carefree days and laughter with Shelly and Bo cascaded over her, bringing a pain that pierced through her.

She stood from the table. "We need to go now." Josh looked at her in surprise. "They've said they have nothing for us." She swallowed against the pain she'd refused to feel for two long years. "Thank you for letting us talk to you. Bo, I'm glad you've found happiness."

She didn't wait for Josh to follow. She raced out of the door and headed for his car, stuffing down the agony that seeing Bo had created.

She was already in the passenger seat when Josh came out of the front door. He got behind the steering wheel and turned to look at her. "Are you all right?"

"No, I'm not. I want to go home. Please just take me home."

"But we'd planned lunch at Jimmy's Place," he protested.

She opened her car door. "Either drive me back to my house or I'll walk. I don't want to see or talk to anyone else today."

"Get in. We'll go back to your place."

She slammed the car door and buckled up. Irrational anger toward Josh combined with the aching grief of loss. It was his fault that she had lost her cocoon of numbness that had served her so well.

Seeing Bo had hurt and reminded her of all she had lost. She didn't want to feel that hurt. She wanted to crawl back into her detachment from people and life.

Chapter Ten

The next day at noon, Josh and Savannah headed for Jimmy's Place for lunch. Savannah had spent much of her time the day before holed up in her bedroom while Josh called Trey to make sure the sheriff checked out not only Eric's alibi for Saturday night but also Chad Wilson. After that he had restlessly roamed the house.

He hadn't considered how difficult it might be for Savannah to see Bo again, but when she did appear for dinner, she seemed angry at Josh. While they'd eaten he'd tried to talk to her about her feelings, but she was having nothing to do with any deep conversations.

She answered him tersely and refused to make eye contact with him. When the kitchen was clean she returned to her bedroom for the remainder of the night.

This morning it had been as if yesterday had never happened. She'd greeted him pleasantly and they'd shared coffee talking about nonthreatening, nonsensical things.

Things had remained light and easy between them until it was time to leave the house. Only then did he feel the tension that rolled off her and knew this outing would be another difficult one for her.

Part of him wanted to coddle her. If she felt most comfortable at home, then that was where she should be. But the stronger part of him believed she needed to get out of the house, start rebuilding a real life for herself.

Josh knew that grief could be a crippling thing, but he also knew she'd carried hers long enough. It was time for her let go and move into acceptance. Shelly was dead, but Savannah was still very much alive.

Each time he saw a spark of the woman she'd once been, he wanted more. He wanted her. No woman had ever stirred him like Savannah did. He'd believed she could be the woman for him two years ago, and he still felt the same way.

"Are you hungry?" he asked as he pulled into the parking area next to Jimmy's Place.

"I can't tell if it's nerves or hunger that's making my stomach jump and kick," she replied.

"Probably a little bit of both." He shut off the engine and turned to look at her. "There's nothing to be afraid of, Savannah. We're in a public place and I've got your back."

"I know. I'm just not used to being around so many people. But let's do this," she said with a tone of resolve and opened her car door.

Jimmy's Place had once been Bo's Place, but when Bo had been accused of Shelly's murder, the patrons of the hugely popular upscale bar and grill had stopped coming. Bo had left town and sold the place to his best friend, Jimmy Tambor.

It was Jimmy who greeted them as they walked in the door. Lanky and slightly awkward, the sandy-haired man smiled even wider as he saw Savannah. "Gosh, Savannah, I haven't seen you in forever. You look terrific. It's great to have you here."

"Thanks, Jimmy."

"Table for two?" he asked and looked at Josh.

Josh nodded, and Jimmy led them away from the bar area and into a dining area, where Josh immediately spied a table full of town officials.

Mayor Jim Burns, former mayor Frank Kean, councilman Neil Sampson and Trey Walker all sat at a long table. With them was Rod Nixon from the amusement park. Trey motioned them over, and Josh immediately felt Savannah stiffen.

Still, she walked next to Josh as he headed for the men. "Savannah," Neil said with a smile. "What a surprise. I've heard you've had a rough time lately."

"I'm fine," she replied tersely.

"I wanted to let you know that I checked out Eric's and Chad's alibis for Saturday night," Trey said to Josh. "Unfortunately both of them claim that they were at home alone all night, and nobody can corroborate their alibis."

"The exciting news is that we've mapped out miles of tunnels," Jim Burns said.

"And they all appear to be solid. We're talking about how to capitalize on the find when we've finished mapping the rest and they all prove safe," Frank Kean added.

"The tunnels add a great feature to the amusement park," Rod added.

Josh nodded. "I'd like to get a copy of whatever map you have," he said to Trey. "I've started my own map, but obviously you all have done a lot more exploring in the last couple of days."

"Stop by my office later this afternoon and I'll give you a copy of what I have," Trey said.

"Will do," Josh replied.

Moments later he and Savannah were seated at a table some distance away from the group. Jimmy took their drink orders and then disappeared.

"Okay, tell me which of those men you don't like or don't trust," Josh said.

She hesitated and unfolded her napkin in her lap. "It's not a matter of trust. I just don't like Neil Sampson. He's an arrogant jerk."

"Does he know you think he's a jerk?" Josh asked.

"Probably, although I've had nothing to do with him for a long time. We dated briefly about three years ago." Her cheeks flushed with a faint pink hue. "He was my first real grown-up relationship." It was easy for Josh to read between the lines. Neil Sampson had been Savannah's first lover.

The conversation halted as Jimmy arrived with their drinks and took their food orders. After he'd left, Savannah continued, the blush still riding her cheeks.

"We'd only dated for about a month when he decided

it was time to get intimate. I didn't really feel ready to take that step with him, but it happened, it wasn't pleasant and after that I stopped seeing him."

"Did he rape you?" Josh asked in a low whisper, his blood starting to boil.

"No," she assured him quickly. "More like coerced, but I didn't tell him no."

It didn't matter. Josh still wanted to smash Neil's handsome face in. "I know he dated Claire for a while, but apparently she didn't find him to her taste, either," Savannah added.

Once again they both fell silent as Jimmy arrived with their food orders. "Neil is very ambitious," Josh said once Jimmy had departed. "I think he's grooming himself to be the next mayor. I wonder if he sees you as a threat to his reputation."

"I wouldn't hurt his reputation by telling anyone that he was a crummy lover who pressured me into having sex with him when I wasn't ready."

"You know that, but does he?" Josh looked across the room at the subject of their discussion. Neil was a good-looking guy who had become Jim Burns's right-hand man. He was also arrogant and gave off an aura of entitlement.

Josh shifted his gaze to the other diners in the place, seeking anyone who appeared to be paying too much attention to Savannah, anyone who seemed to radiate any animus. While the place was fairly filled with lunch diners, Josh didn't notice anyone or anything odd.

Josh attacked his burger. "Did you know that Shelly was having doubts about marrying Bo?" he asked after a couple of bites.

Savannah frowned with a french fry in her fingers. "I know that Shelly loved Bo, but she wanted out of Lost Lagoon so badly, and Bo had built up his business and had his mother here. He wasn't going to leave, and if she hadn't died I think she wouldn't have stayed here and married Bo."

She popped the fry into her mouth and then took a drink of her soda. "She told me before her death that she had a sticky situation to deal with and even though she wouldn't go into any details with me, I think that situation had to do with the decision she had to make where Bo was concerned. I still don't see how what happened to Shelly has anything to do with what is going on with me."

"I agree," Josh replied. "I think we can put that piece of the puzzle behind us. It just doesn't fit."

He looked again at the table of town bigwigs, his focus yet again on Neil Sampson. Had Savannah downplayed what had happened between them years ago? Had their intimate encounter been more of a rape than she'd indicated?

If so, then Neil could potentially see Savannah as a risk to his grand ambitions. Rumor was that he not only wanted to become mayor but also had intentions of eventually entering politics in a bigger way.

The fact that she had been a virtual recluse for the past two years might have lulled him into a sense of safety.

He had certainly learned of the attack on her in the tunnels, and that might have made him realize if she left her isolated lifestyle, if she started to talk to people, then she might tell somebody about what had happened between them.

That would definitely besmirch the stellar reputation he'd worked so hard to build for himself over the past couple of years.

It smelled like a potential motive to Josh.

FIVE DAYS LATER, on Sunday afternoon, Savannah worked in the kitchen preparing a mandarin orange, bacon and spinach salad, beef Wellington and new potatoes in a garlic butter sauce.

She had talked Josh into spending the day in after the past week of socializing and visiting nearly every storefront and person in Lost Lagoon.

He now sat at the kitchen table with the newest tunnel map that Trey had provided him the day before. "If these tunnels were really made by pirates, then they made sure they had plenty of escape routes."

Savannah left her work at the counter and moved to the table to peer over his shoulder. "It looks like a colorful mess to me."

She was acutely aware of the scent of him that had become so familiar in the last week. It was a fragrance that evoked memories of the kiss they had shared and that moment when she'd seen him in the bathroom clad only in a white towel.

She stepped back and returned to the counter and

her cooking. She was becoming far too comfortable in Josh's company. He made her laugh and he made her think. He fascinated her with his stories of his childhood and what it was like to be a twin.

With each day that passed, she felt him getting beneath her defenses. They had developed a domestic intimacy that had her thinking about how things could be if she would only allow him into her heart.

She'd been half in love with him before Shelly's murder. She was walking that same path now, trying to fight against it but feeling she was losing the battle.

It had even become easier each day for her to leave the house and interact with other people in town.

She'd forgotten how many friends Shelly had before her death, friends who had also been Savannah's. As she met up with them, she was fascinated to learn who was dating whom, who had gotten engaged and all the girl gossip she'd missed for the past two years.

Seeing those people again hadn't been as painful as she'd expected. In fact, there had been a lot of laughter and warmth.

She knew Josh was keeping in close phone contact with Trey concerning the attacks on her, but the official investigation had come to a screeching halt, as had Josh and her unofficial investigation.

Josh had made it clear that he had three potential suspects on his short list: Eric Baptiste, Chad Wilson and Neil Sampson.

He believed Eric might be involved in something

illegal in the tunnels and was now angry that Savannah had told about the tunnels.

He also believed it possible that Chad had some crazy crush on her and now wanted some revenge because she hadn't shown any romantic interest in him.

Finally, he believed it was possible Neil just wanted to silence Savannah forever so she wouldn't be a threat to any future political ambitions he might entertain.

She found it difficult to believe any of those men had been behind the attacks on her, but she also believed that Shelly's killer had walked the streets of the small town for two long years and probably appeared to be a nice, pleasant man that nobody would ever suspect of being capable of murder.

She was particularly aware of Josh this evening. She found comfort in him seated at her table, a sense that he belonged there for every dinner and for every morning cup of coffee. Dangerous thoughts, she reminded herself as she crushed garlic that filled the air with its pungent odor.

Josh was here to protect her from a threat she was beginning to believe might already be over. Nothing had happened over the past week to shake her up. Nobody had acted odd or displayed anything but delight at seeing her out and around town.

Equally dangerous thoughts, she told herself. She shouldn't be lulled into a false sense of safety just because it had been a quiet week.

"There are a couple of tunnels off the main one that you used that still haven't been explored," he said, breaking into her thoughts. "Maybe you and I should go down and check them out."

She turned once again to look at him. God, he was so handsome with his dark hair slightly mussed and a gleam of intelligent concentration in his eyes. He was dressed in a pair of jeans and a light blue T-shirt that hugged the breadth of his shoulders.

"I'll be honest with you. I don't think I can go down in the tunnels again," she confessed. "Even the thought of it closes off my throat and makes me feel like I might have a panic attack."

"That's okay," he replied with an easy smile. "It was just a thought, but we can leave it up to the others to finish mapping the pathways."

He folded the map and shoved it to the side. "What's for dinner? You've been working on it for a while now." She told him her menu and he released a low whistle. "If you keep feeding me this great food each night, I might never want to leave."

And that was the problem. She was beginning to think she didn't want him to ever leave. The silence of the house that she'd once found so comforting had been banished by Josh's presence.

They spent each evening after dinner with a glass of wine in the living room, where they talked about the little things that built a relationship.

She knew his favorite color was blue, that he loved his work here but would eventually like to get on the day shift. She learned his mother's name was Rose and his father was Rick, and she had shared some of her pain over the desertion of her own parents after her sister's death. That had become her favorite time of their day together, when they sat on the sofa and shared pieces of themselves.

She jumped as the doorbell rang.

Josh was on his feet with his gun in his hand in a second. "I'm assuming you aren't expecting anyone," he said.

"Definitely not," she replied.

"I'll answer the door. You stay here," he instructed her. He disappeared from the kitchen. A moment later he returned with Savannah's brother trailing behind him. Mac Sinclair was a big man with an imposing build. He had the Sinclair dark hair and brown eyes and always radiated irritation that bordered on an explosion of anger.

"Mac," Savannah said in surprise. "What are you doing here?"

"Sheila thinks the lamp in my old bedroom will look perfect in our bedroom, so I've come to get it."

This had been a common occurrence since their parents had left the house and Mac had married and set up his own home. He'd already taken the gas grill, a recliner and sundry other items. It was as if when he needed to shop for something he just came here and took what he wanted.

"But it looks nice where it is," she protested and trailed after him as he headed down the hallway. "And Josh is using that room right now." Josh remained in the living room, obviously deciding not to get involved in a sibling argument. "Why don't you just go buy your own lamp?"

They entered the bedroom where the pretty silver lamp sat on one of the nightstands. "Everything in this house is half mine," he replied. "You're lucky I'm just taking a lamp and not the sofa or something else. Besides, I doubt if Josh is doing any reading at night."

He yanked the plug from the wall and picked up the lamp. Savannah wanted to protest but decided an argument with her hot-headed, mean-tempered brother over a lamp wasn't worth it. There was another lamp in the small locked spare room if Josh needed it.

She followed him back down to the living room, where Josh stood waiting. "Josh," Mac said as if noticing him for the first time.

"Mac," Josh returned coolly.

"I heard through the grapevine that you were on babysitting duty," Mac said.

"Your sister is hardly a baby," Josh replied evenly, but his jaw bunched in a ticking knot.

"Just take the lamp and go, Mac," Savannah said. She didn't want to hear her brother degrade her or Josh defend her. She just wanted to get back to the peace she'd felt before her brother had shown up for one of his occasional raids.

Once Mac had left, she and Josh returned to the kitchen. She went back to the counter to continue her dinner preparations, and Josh sat back at the table.

Dinner was a success. The beef Wellington came out perfectly, as did everything else she had prepared.

The conversation flowed easily, and it was just after seven when the kitchen was cleaned up and they each carried a glass of wine to the living room.

As usual, he sat on one side of the sofa and she sat on the other. Now that they were out of the kitchen with the cooking smells, she could smell him, that heady scent of clean male and spice-laden cologne.

"I'm probably going to gain a hundred pounds during my time here," he said and patted his flat abdomen.

"You'll gain way more weight eating George's greasy burgers or all that fried food at Jimmy's Place," she replied, but his words had pulled forth that erotic picture of him in the towel, the sculptured bulk of his magnificent body on display.

They sipped their wine in a comfortable silence for a few moments. "Does Mac come by often and just take what he wants from here?" he asked.

"Often enough," she admitted.

"Do you always let him take what he wants so easily?"

A knot twisted in her stomach as she thought of her older brother. "Most of the time. To be fair, the house was left to both of us when Mom and Dad left town. He could have forced me to sell and split the cash, but thankfully he's let me stay here, so if he wants to take some things from here, I don't argue with him much. There's an extra lamp in the spare room if you need one next to your bed."

"Nah, I'm fine with just the overhead light," he replied.

She took another sip of her wine, the knot in her

stomach twisting tighter. "Sometimes I wonder..." she let her voice trail off, unsure she could speak aloud the haunting thoughts she'd entertained for the last two years.

"You wonder about what?" Josh placed his wineglass on the coffee table and moved closer to her on the sofa.

Savannah set her wineglass down as well, gazing at Josh intently. "Sometimes I wonder if it was Mac who killed Shelly." The knot inside her eased as she finally spoke of the secret thought she'd held inside for so long.

Chapter Eleven

Josh stared at her in surprise. "Why on earth would you think that?"

Her eyes misted with sudden emotion. "I don't want to believe it. You're the first person I've ever told, but for the last two years I've often wondered."

"Why would Mac kill Shelly?" Mac's name had never come up in the initial investigation. He'd appeared nothing more than a grieving brother at the time.

"Mac hated Bo. He didn't think Bo was good enough for Shelly. He didn't say too much when Bo and Shelly were dating in high school, but as their relationship continued on, Mac was on Shelly's back all the time to break up with Bo. When they finally got engaged, Mac was livid. He tried every way possible to get Shelly to break off the engagement, to get her away from Bo."

The mist in her eyes had become pools as she continued, "I don't think he meant to kill her, but Shelly gave as good as she got from Mac. When he yelled at her, she'd yell louder. While I was always a little bit afraid of Mac and his temper, Shelly never was."

"And so you think it was Mac she met that night at the stone bench down by the swamp?"

"If Mac had asked her to meet him there at that time of night, she probably wouldn't have thought twice about it. I believe it's possible Mac tried to talk Shelly into breaking up with Bo, and things got out of hand between them. It's possible Mac's temper got the best of him. I don't believe he killed her on purpose, but maybe they got into a tussle and Shelly wound up dead, and Mac stole the engagement ring as if to have the final say."

Twin tears trekked down her cheeks and she shook her head and gave a forced laugh. "I must sound crazy. Sometimes I feel like I'm crazy even to consider such a scenario. Most days I don't believe it's possible that he had anything to do with the murder, but other days I can't help but wonder."

Josh's heart squeezed tight at the sight of her tears. "Do you really believe that your brother is capable of killing your sister?"

"That's just it. I don't know. All I know for sure is that the wrong man was accused and that the killer is still walking free." She waved her hand as if to dismiss the topic, but tears ran faster down her face, and Josh could stand it no longer.

He reached out to her, and she came into his arms. She cried only a brief time and then raised her head to gaze at him. "I don't want to believe that Mac is capable of such a thing. I just wish I knew who killed Shelly and who wants me dead."

Josh swept several strands of her silken hair away from her face. "I wish I could give you the answers to all of your questions," he said softly. Then he did what he'd desperately wanted to do for the past week. He kissed her.

Rather than shying away from him, she leaned into him, opening her mouth to allow him to kiss her deeply, soulfully. Just feeling the heat, the softness of her lips, turned him on full force.

However, he had no intention of taking it any further unless she initiated it. He knew what he wanted, but he cared enough about her that it had to be on her terms or not at all.

As she continued to cling to him, as the kiss deepened and went on, he was conscious of every soft curve pressed against him, the heady scent of her that swirled in his head and increased his want.

She finally broke the kiss, her eyes dark and glazed with a desire that fed his own. "Make love to me, Josh."

He looked deep into her beautiful eyes, seeking any doubt she might have after what she'd just asked of him. He saw none, and when she stood and pulled him up off the sofa, his heart pounded with sweet anticipation.

He'd wanted her two years ago, and spending this past week with her had been more than a little bit of torture as he fought against his desire for her. That desire now roared through him as she led him to her bedroom. The bed was neatly made, and he scarcely got inside the door before she wrapped her arms around his neck and pulled him tightly against her as she sought his lips for another kiss.

He didn't hesitate to comply. He took possession of her mouth as he tangled his hands in her long silky hair. She molded her body to his and moved her hips just enough to set him on fire.

The spill of illumination from the hallway was the only light in the room, but it was enough for him to see her beautiful features as she broke the kiss and stepped away from him.

He stood perfectly still, watching her walk to the opposite side of the bed and pull down the spread to display pale pink sheets.

He stopped breathing as she reached down, grabbed the bottom of her T-shirt and pulled it up and over her head, revealing bare skin and a lacy bra. He still didn't breathe when she kicked off her sandals, unzipped and stepped out of her capris and then got into bed and covered up with a sheet.

"Aren't you going to join me?" she asked, a sexy huskiness in her voice.

He finally breathed, drawing in a deep gulp of air as he sprang into action. He yanked off his T-shirt and stepped out of his shoes. His socks followed, and he nearly fell over getting out of his jeans.

The minute he got into bed and under the sheet, he was surrounded by the scent of her, a fragrance he never wanted to get out of his head.

Their bodies came together at the same time they

kissed once again. He marveled at the softness of her skin, the fire in her kiss.

He'd wanted her to come alive, to feel, to be more present, and she was definitely present in this moment. She stroked down his bare back, and at the same time he reached beneath her to unfasten her bra.

When he had it unhooked, she moved her shoulders to allow him to pluck it off her. He pulled his mouth from hers and instead began to blaze a trail of kisses down the length of her neck.

She grabbed his hair, and a gasp escaped her as he covered one of her nipples with his mouth and used his tongue to lick it into a hard pebble.

She moaned his name. He moved to her other breast, taking his time to give her the most pleasure. He wanted this to be an experience she would never forget, a gentle, tender loving that would banish whatever Neil Sampson might have done to her.

He wanted to brand her as his, to make it impossible for her ever to want to make love to any other man. It was with this thought that he recognized the depth of his love for Savannah Sinclair.

A HAZE OF pleasure swept over Savannah, a pleasure she had never known before. His hands and mouth moved over her body in a languid fashion, as if he were in no hurry to finish.

He held his weight on his elbows as he slowly kissed down her stomach to the edge of her panties and then back up again. Her entire body pulsed with need, a new feeling for her.

She'd wanted him since they'd shared their first kiss, since she'd seen him in that low-slung towel, but she couldn't believe she'd made the brazen request that he follow through on giving her what she wanted.

She'd known he wouldn't deny her. She'd felt his desire for her almost every moment they had spent together. She was thirty years old and had experienced sex only once before, with Neil Sampson. And what she'd gone through with him wasn't even remotely close to what was happening now with Josh.

Josh was focused solely on her pleasure, and oh, what pleasure he brought her. When one of his hands slid down her stomach and over the silk of her panties, she instinctively moved her hips up to meet his touch.

Her silk panties became hot, an irritating barrier she wanted gone. As if he read her mind, his thumbs hooked on either side and he slowly pulled them down, moving his body as he tugged them down her legs and off her feet.

Her heart pounded and her breathing became even more rapid as he crawled back up and captured her lips with his. At the same time, his hand slipped down to touch her where her panties no longer shielded her.

His fingers found her most sensitive spot and began to rub back and forth in a rhythm that swelled up sensations inside her, sensations that climbed higher and higher, until she could stand no more.

Her release crashed through her, along with an

uninhibited gasp of laughter and a surprising sob. She gazed up at him in wonder, having never experienced that kind of sexual fever and overwhelming loss of control before.

"Can you do that to me again?" she asked breathlessly.

He laughed and kissed her cheek. "I can definitely try."

And he did. Twice more she rode the waves of intense climaxes, and after the last one, while she was still gasping and boneless, he slid off his boxers and positioned himself between her thighs and entered her.

He remained unmoving, as if making sure she was comfortable. She was more than comfortable. Her entire body was on fire. She wrapped her arms around his back, wanting to keep him that close to her forever. He began to move his hips against hers, and they quickly found a rhythm that stole her breath away and forced all thoughts out of her head.

There was just Josh, filling her, surrounding her and kissing her with a tender passion as their bodies moved in unison.

She was shocked when the waves of sensation began to build yet again, sweeping her up in an intense sensual haze that washed over her. At the same time she felt him stiffen and moan her name as he found his own release.

They remained interlocked for several long minutes, too breathless to move, neither willing to break their intimate connection. "That was better than amazing," he finally said.

"That was better than awesome," she replied with a smile.

"I don't even think there's a word in the English language to describe what it was." He stroked her cheek with his thumb, and for a brief moment, in the faint light of the room, she saw a raw, vulnerable emotion in his eyes.

It was there only a moment and then gone. She tried to convince herself she'd just imagined it. It had just been a trick of the light. That look of pure love had been nothing but her imagination.

He leaned down and kissed the tip of her nose, then rolled from the bed and to his feet. "I'll be right back," he said.

He padded naked out of the room, and Savannah stared up at the ceiling, thinking about what had just happened. She'd never known that making love could be such exquisite pleasure.

The night she'd spent with Neil had been filled with pain and shame. Josh had given her something far different. Josh had given her pure and unadulterated pleasure. He'd gifted her with sweetness and gentleness that had touched not only her body but also her soul. Her body still hummed with a contented relaxation she hadn't felt in years, perhaps had never felt before.

He returned to the room, smelling of soap, with his gun in hand. It was obvious he meant to sleep with her for the rest of the night.

"My turn," she said and slid from the bed. She hurried into the bathroom. She knew it was a bad idea to allow him to sleep with her, but the idea of having him right next to her in bed for the entire night was both provocative and comforting.

One night, she told herself as she left the bathroom and headed back to her bedroom. One night of lovemaking and one night of sleeping together and that would be the end of it.

She couldn't afford to let it happen again. She didn't have the desire or the strength to love anyone again. But for just this single night, she'd let go of her fear and allow herself to feel. Then tomorrow she could crawl back into her cocoon of isolation and self-protection.

She was grateful that when she got back into bed, he didn't seem inclined to talk. He just pulled her close to him, close enough that she thought she could feel his heartbeat against her own.

When she was almost asleep, she turned over with Josh spooned around her back, his breath warming the back of her neck. Nice, she thought. So nice…and that was her last thought.

When she awakened the next morning, she was in bed alone.

The smell of frying bacon and fresh brewed coffee drifted down the hallway from the kitchen. She rolled onto her back and stared up at the ceiling, where the morning sunshine danced through a slit in the curtains.

Instead of stretching like a satisfied cat, she turned back on her side and curled into a fetal ball. Mistake…

As magnificent as last night had been, it had been a huge mistake.

She knew that Josh had a romantic interest in her, and last night had to have given him all the wrong impressions. She thought of that moment when she'd believed she'd seen raw love pouring from his eyes.

It had awed her. It had frightened her. She didn't want him to love her, and she definitely didn't want to love him. He'd already forced her out of her home and into town, something she hadn't wanted to do. She'd been like a snail, perfectly happy and safe in her little shell, but he'd pushed and pulled her out into the dangerous world of emotional vulnerability once again.

It had been over a week since the attack on her at the inn, and nothing more dangerous had happened to her than a hangnail. There were long periods of time as she and Josh were just walking the streets of Lost Lagoon when she forgot that somebody wanted her dead.

In fact, there were long periods when she was with Josh that she forgot to be unhappy and didn't think about her grief or the loss of her sister.

It felt like a betrayal to Shelly, as if she were on the verge of forgetting one of the most important, most beloved persons in her life.

She finally unfurled and got out of bed. She grabbed her nightgown, pulled it over her head, topped it with her robe and headed for the bathroom, where she brushed her teeth, washed her face and pulled a brush through her hair.

She felt unaccountably shy about seeing Josh this

morning. He'd not only given her sexual pleasure she'd never known existed but also been like a warm, comforting blanket she'd snuggled into as she'd fallen asleep.

With a final flick of the brush through her hair, she set the brush down and left the bathroom. She heard him before she reached the kitchen. He was singing a popular tune slightly off-key but with cheerful enthusiasm.

He stood at the oven, using a spatula to stir scrambled eggs in her iron skillet. He was clad only in a pair of jeans, looking hot with his bare torso and totally at ease and at home with his bare feet.

"Good morning," she said.

He jumped and turned around with dismay creasing his forehead. "Shoot, I was going to serve you breakfast in bed this morning."

"That's sweet, but I'm up now." She walked over to the counter with the coffeemaker and poured herself a cup. "But you can serve me at the table."

"It's just not the same," he replied with a pretend pout. He whirled back around as the toaster popped. She sat at the table and watched in amusement as he tried to juggle buttering the toast and taking the eggs from the skillet and getting it all, along with the bacon, on two plates.

He set her plate in front of her and then sat down across the table with his own. "I was going to make you pancakes, but I didn't see any pancake mix in your pantry."

"I don't use a mix when I make pancakes," she replied. She was grateful that, other than his breakfast-making, things appeared normal between them.

She just hoped she could make him understand without hurting him that last night was a one-time deal and wasn't going to be repeated.

As they ate, he talked about the different kinds of pancakes his mother used to make when he was young. Once again Savannah was struck by the domesticity of the scene.

What scared her was that she'd grown accustomed to sharing breakfast with him, eating lunch out and returning home to cook him a good dinner. They had been living like a married couple, and it was all too easy for her to fantasize about it continuing on forever.

It was time to pull away from him, to distance herself from the life she knew he could…he might offer to her. She knew he was here to protect her, but the lines had become blurred between them.

She was no longer a victim waiting for an attack. She felt as if she were a woman who'd already been attacked…by a love she refused to acknowledge, a love she didn't want to embrace.

It was definitely time to withdraw, to crawl back into her shell of safety where she didn't feel, where grief and heartache could never touch her again.

Chapter Twelve

By Tuesday afternoon, Josh knew that Savannah had gone back to the woman she had been when he'd first caught her crawling out of the hole in her backyard.

Throughout the day before, as they'd gone into town and eaten lunch at Jimmy's Place, she had been quiet and withdrawn, as if she wanted to be anyplace else but out with him.

He'd tried to start several conversations but had finally given up when she hadn't responded to any of his attempts. He could only guess that their lovemaking had scared her, while it had emboldened him.

He was in love with her, and that night had only solidified what he already knew. He wanted to build a life with her, have children with her and have her embrace life and happiness once again. He'd thought their night together had been the beginning of all of that happening.

But it had become obvious that for her, that night had been the end of anything between them. Fear and grief once again clung to her, and this fed his frustration.

Over the last two weeks, he'd seen her laughter. He'd felt love flowing from her. He'd seen the potential future with her in it, and he'd liked what he saw.

But this morning, she'd stayed in bed during the time they normally shared breakfast. Then, when she'd finally gotten up and he'd mentioned heading out into town for the afternoon, she'd refused to go. Instead she'd returned to her bedroom and he hadn't seen her since.

He'd made several phone calls, talking to Daniel for a while to get his take on the investigation into the attacks on Savannah, and then calling Trey to get an update.

An hour ago, Ray McClure had run by a copy of the most recent map of the tunnels. Josh had pored over the map, finding it interesting that Trey, the mayor and whoever else was involved had been working backward from the swamp, leaving several of the tunnels closest to Savannah's house still unexplored.

Once again his concern was that Trey was far more interested in the tunnels than he was in solving any crime or helping to protect Savannah.

He'd finally rolled up the map and carried it into the guest room where he'd been staying. He returned to the kitchen, surprised to find Savannah there, rummaging in the refrigerator.

"I had a ham and cheese sandwich for lunch," he said. "There's still plenty left if you want one."

"Thanks." She pulled out the packages of ham and cheese and a jar of mayo. He sat at the table and watched as she made her sandwich, wondering if she intended to take it back to her bedroom to eat.

He was ridiculously pleased when she carried her plate to the table and sat across from him. She took several bites and chased them with drinks of sweet tea.

She didn't speak, nor did she look at him. She kept her gaze focused on her plate as if he wasn't in the room at all. His frustration grew. He felt as if she was punishing him for a decision that had been her own.

He hadn't taken her down the hallway to the bedroom to make love to her. She'd been in charge of the whole thing, and now she acted like he was the one at fault.

"Nice day," he said, breaking the silence.

"Who cares?" she replied.

He leaned back in his chair and released a deep sigh. "What's going on, Savannah?"

She finally looked at him, her eyes dark and fathomless. "This isn't working for me." She pushed away her plate with her half-eaten sandwich.

"What isn't working?" he asked, wondering if she wanted something else to eat.

"This…" She pointed to herself and then to him. "You being here. We haven't learned anything worthwhile about who attacked me. Nothing else has happened to make me think I'm in imminent danger."

"That's because I'm here," he countered.

"I'll call Buck Ranier this afternoon and have him install a security system that rings right into the sheriff's station. I'll be safe here alone, and you can go back to your own life and work."

Josh stared at her in disbelief. "Is this because of what happened between us the other night?"

She looked away from him. "No...yes, partly," she replied. She released a sigh and looked at him once again. "I know you care about me, Josh."

"I'm in love with you, Savannah." He hadn't meant to tell her like this, not under these circumstances, but now that he'd spoken the words aloud, the depth of his love for her filled his heart.

Her eyes were huge. "I don't want you to be in love with me."

He released a dry laugh. "You don't get to be in charge of how I feel about you. I love you and I want to build a future with you. I want you to have my babies and sleep in my arms every night for the rest of our lives."

She raised her chin and her lips trembled slightly. "I might not be in charge of what you want, but I get to be in charge of whether you're welcome here or not, and you're no longer welcome here."

"So, you're kicking me out?" He stared at her in stunned shock.

"That's exactly what I'm doing," she replied.

Josh's frustration exploded. "Why? So you can crawl back into the hole of darkness you've been in for the past two years? So you can wallow in your grief forever instead of accepting that a terrible thing happened to your sister, but you're still very much alive? You staying miserable and isolated won't change anything, Savannah. Shelly is dead, and you've been her ghost for too long."

She got up from her chair and stepped back from the table. "Shelly was murdered, and you and all the rest of your buddies didn't do anything to find her real killer. You pinned it on Bo because it was the easy thing to do, but you didn't conduct a real investigation."

Her words pierced through Josh's very soul. He wanted to deny them, to protest her assessment violently, but he couldn't. She was right. Dammit, she was right, and he couldn't do anything to change what had happened two years ago.

"Maybe you don't love me at all," she continued. "Maybe you just feel guilty about what you didn't do for Shelly."

This brought him up out of his chair. "Trust me, Savannah. I know the difference between guilt and love, and while I will always regret not pursuing the investigation into Shelly's death more thoroughly at the time, guilt has nothing to do with me loving you."

He took a step toward her, but she backed away from him. "I don't want you to love me, and I don't want to love you," she replied, her voice louder than usual. "And you're wrong that I've been stuck in grief for the past two years. I've been in a safe place where I've felt nothing, and that's the way I like it."

"What about happiness? Don't you want to be happy, Savannah? Don't you want to feel and give love, to have children and build a life of happiness?"

He gazed at her and knew his heart was in his eyes for her to see.

She looked away from him. "I'm happy alone, and that's why it's time for you to leave. I told you I'd call Buck and arrange for security. That's all I need." She looked at him once again, and tears shone in her eyes. "I don't need you and I don't want you here anymore. Please just go."

He stared at her, stunned by what she was saying and unable to do anything except what she asked. He wasn't here in any legal capacity. Officially he was on vacation, making him just a guest in her home... apparently an unwanted guest.

"Okay, I'll go," he finally said, because he couldn't legally do anything else.

He'd leave for a couple of hours, give her some time to be alone and maybe cool down. Then he'd come back, and hopefully they could have a rational discussion instead of the emotionally charged one that had just taken place.

He already had his gun around his waist, but he refused to go into the bedroom and pack his things. He refused to accept that this was the end of things. He didn't want to believe that she didn't love him and that love wouldn't eventually win.

He left the kitchen and headed for the front door, aware of her following him. When he reached the door he turned to look at her. "Are you positive this is what you want?"

She hesitated a moment and then nodded. "It's exactly what I want."

"Shelly's funeral should have been a double one," he said. "Because when she was buried, you gave up on life. You're a dead woman walking."

He didn't wait for her response but turned and walked out of the front door. Myriad thoughts flew through his head as he went to his car.

He looked around the neighborhood to see if anything or anyone appeared unusual but saw nothing. It wouldn't be unusual for Josh's car to leave Savannah's driveway in the middle of the day, either. There was no reason for anyone to believe she was in the house alone. Everyone would just assume she was with him in the car someplace in town.

He didn't even want to think about the ache that resounded in his heart over the heated words they'd exchanged, words in which she'd denied any love for him in her heart.

He believed in his heart that she did love him, but he couldn't make her admit it, and he certainly couldn't make her act on it. She was determined to stay in a state of limbo between life and death, and until she decided to make a change, his efforts on her behalf would be fruitless.

He'd give her a couple of hours to cool down. In the meantime, he decided he might do a little tunnel exploration on his own. When he returned, he had to convince her somehow that he could be her bodyguard and nothing more, because the most important thing to him, no matter how she chose to live her life, was that she had a life to live.

THE MINUTE HE walked out the door, Savannah crumpled on the sofa in tears. Agonizing waves of emotion swept over her, the very emotions she'd spent two years attempting not to feel.

He was in love with her. He wanted to build a future with her, and she'd just told him to get out of her life. She was in love with him, but she was afraid to invite him into her heart.

And for several tormenting moments, she wondered what she truly was afraid of. After Shelly's death, she had never wanted to feel again, to love or care about anything or anyone again.

But for the last couple of weeks, Josh had pulled her back to life, had forced her to find her laughter and a joy she hadn't experienced since Shelly's murder.

She had a feeling it would be impossible for her to go back to the ghost she had been. Josh had breathed life and love into her heart, which was why she had to send him away. She was afraid of everything he held out in a tantalizingly close hand.

She finally wiped away her tears and got up from the sofa. She grabbed her cell phone and looked up the number for Buck's Security Systems. She hoped he could come right over and get something installed by nightfall.

She knew eventually Josh would be back, if for no other reason than to pick up the clothes he had left behind. But she'd accused him of slacking in Shelly's murder investigation, which was hitting below the belt.

She couldn't blame Josh for what she considered a

shoddy investigation into Shelly's murder. He'd had to follow the orders of Trey, and Trey had truly believed Bo guilty.

Still, she had no idea how angry she might have made Josh by blaming him. Maybe it was good if she made him angry. Then he'd want to keep his distance from her.

Thankfully the phone call to Buck resulted in the older man telling her he'd arrive within the hour to get her set up with the most updated security system he installed.

While she waited for Buck to arrive, she threw away her half-eaten sandwich and placed the plate in the dishwasher. She then scrubbed down the countertops and shone the wood of the cabinet fronts, needing the physical activity to keep her from thinking.

She didn't want to think anymore. She didn't want to replay Josh's words of love in her head. She didn't want to worry about some creep trying to kill her. She just wished for mindlessness.

She was grateful when Buck finally arrived with his utility truck filled with goodies to keep her safe and sound in the house. She unlocked the doors to the master suite and the extra bedroom that she and Josh had locked up on the first day he'd arrived.

"I'm assuming you want every window and every door covered," Buck said as he walked around the house to check it out.

"And security cameras at the front and back doors," she replied.

"Then I'd better get started." He walked out to his truck, and Savannah sat in a chair in the living room. He returned with all kinds of wire and items Savannah didn't recognize. She only knew they would keep her safe from harm while she was alone in the house.

She wasn't really concerned about being safe during the daytime hours. She just wanted the added protection for when night fell. It was in the dark of night when she'd been attacked at the inn and when she'd seen somebody peeking in her window. It was in the darkness that she felt most vulnerable.

By four o'clock, Buck had every window and every door in the house wired not only to sound an alarm that would awaken the entire neighborhood but also to ring dispatch at the sheriff's station.

He'd also shown her how to monitor her front and back cameras from her computer, allowing her to see about a three-foot radius around both doors.

It was just after four thirty when he left, and Savannah told herself she felt as safe as if Josh was sitting next to her with his gun.

She fixed herself an omelet for dinner and sat at the kitchen table to eat it, pretending to herself that she liked the silence of the house without Josh's presence.

She'd gotten halfway through the omelet when she saw Trey Walker at her back door. She got up from the table, wondering what the sheriff would be doing here. His updates, what few there had been, had always come through Josh.

Maybe he finally had news for her. Maybe he'd discovered the identity of the attacker and was here to tell her the danger was over.

She punched in the numbers to disarm the security system and then opened the door to allow him inside. "Trey, what's going on?"

His eyes shone with excitement. "You've got to come with me. I think I've figured out the answer to everything, but there is something you need to see."

"What?" she asked eagerly.

"I can't explain it. I have to show it to you." He took her by the arm and led her out the door. When she realized they were headed to the bush…to the hole in the ground that led to the tunnel, she dug in her heels.

"Trey, I don't want to go into the tunnels," she protested. "Just tell me what you found."

"It will just be for a minute," he assured her and pulled her forward at the same time he turned on a flashlight.

"Really, Trey, I never want to go down in the tunnels again." She yanked her arm free from his grasp.

Trey pulled his gun and pointed it at her. "I'm afraid I must insist, Savannah."

She stared at the sheriff, her heart pounding with fear. "What are you doing, Trey?"

"I'm taking care of business," he replied. "And if you get down there and think about running, I'll shoot you in the back." There was no hesitation, no emotion in the flatness of his cold eyes. "Now let's go." He gestured to the hole.

With her mind reeling and her heart beating so fast she was half breathless, Savannah started down the three stairs that led into the tunnel.

Chapter Thirteen

When Josh left Savannah's place, he didn't go home.
He called Trey and got his answering message. Josh
left a message telling him he was taking a break from
Savannah's house and would be back there before dark.

Instead he drove into town and to Mama Baptiste's
shop. From his trunk he grabbed a flashlight. Once
inside the shop, he bought a package of colored chalk.

"I'm using your tunnel entrance," he said to the
older woman as he paid for the chalk. "Where is Eric?
I don't want any surprises when I go in."

Mama Baptiste's dark eyes flashed with irritation.
"My son would never hurt you or anyone else. But you
don't have to worry about him being down in the tunnels. He's at home sick today."

"Do you mind?" Josh pointed toward the back room
where the tunnel entrance was located.

"Who am I to mind? I'm just a shopkeeper. You're
the law," she replied.

Within minutes Josh was in the tunnel and headed
for the main passageway Savannah had always used for

her ghost walks. He had a mental picture of the latest map Trey had provided him in his head.

Trey and his cohorts had been working from the swamp toward town to map the maze of tunnels, but Josh wanted to check out the last two that were branches from the main path that Savannah had used.

Savannah. His heart ached with thoughts of her. It was obvious his love wasn't enough to make her want to embrace life once again. He'd seen so many glimmers of vibrancy from her, when her eyes had shone with passion and caring, when her laughter had filled the air. He'd had such hope for her, for them, but now that hope was gone.

There was no way he intended to leave her in the house alone at night even if she did have a security system installed. It had been his experience that it was in the dark of night that bad things happened, when neighbors were asleep and couldn't witness, when shadows hid the coming and going of criminals.

He felt she'd be safe this afternoon. People would believe she was out with him and not at home. They had established habits over the last two weeks that would make anyone assume that they were together.

He finally reached the main passage and the steps that would lead up to Savannah's backyard. He turned and passed the first two branches that he knew had been explored and mapped thoroughly.

The third branch was the one where Savannah had been attacked. It had been explored until it forked, and then only the left fork had been followed to the end.

When he came to the fork he went right and began to mark his passage with a bright purple piece of chalk.

It appeared to be just another hole in the earth, no secrets, no hidden gold and no reason for somebody to protect this passageway by attacking Savannah.

He hesitated when he reached a second fork. Left or right? If his internal direction was right, the left fork would take him closer to the swamp while the right one would take him more toward the center of town.

He took the right one, continuing to mark his progress with the chalk. The last thing he wanted was to be down here alone and somehow get lost.

Shining the light on his watch, he saw that it was just after four. He wanted to make sure he was up and out of here long before dark. Even if Savannah wanted him out of the house, if necessary he'd stay in his car in her driveway to assure her safety through the days and nights.

He could have sworn she was in love with him. He'd seen it in her eyes, felt it in her touch. But he'd never considered that she might hold such resentment toward him about Shelly's murder investigation, that maybe her resentment might be bigger, deeper than any love.

He quickened his pace, the only sound the echo of his footsteps. He paused only occasionally to mark his path. What he hoped was that by the time he returned to Savannah's, she would have cooled down and realized that, with or without a security system, him being there was the best way to keep her safe.

Although it would be difficult for him, he'd promise her bodyguard behavior and nothing more personal. The rage that had been expended the night she'd been in the inn confused him. Normally a person holding on to that kind of rage wouldn't be able to contain it for over a week.

He was surprised that something else hadn't happened, that the person had managed to keep control for so long. He wasn't sure if his presence in her home was thwarting another attack or if the person was just patiently waiting it out.

Josh couldn't spend the rest of his life on vacation and protecting Savannah. In fact, the last time he'd spoken to Trey, his boss had asked him when he'd be back on regular duty, and Josh hadn't had a definitive answer.

As he'd walked, he'd felt the descent of the ground taking him deeper and deeper. His heart began to pound when he came to the end of the passageway and saw a set of wooden steps built to take somebody upside. The stairs looked relatively new and solid.

Somebody had gone to a lot of trouble to make this tunnel entrance easily accessible. At the top of the stairs was an ordinary door.

He pulled his gun, as always wary as to what he might be walking into. He placed his flashlight on the top stair and then grabbed the doorknob, surprised when it turned easily beneath his grip.

The door opened without a groan or a creak, and he grabbed his flashlight once again as he walked into total darkness. A quick sweep of the light made him guess that he was in somebody's garage, and the utter silence told him he was alone.

He found a light switch on the wall and turned it on. The space felt oddly familiar, with a seed spreader hung on a rack on the wall and a red riding lawnmower parked on one side.

It was only when he looked at the shelves on the opposite side of the space that his breath caught in his throat. Stacks of plastic-wrapped white substance filled the shelves, and next to one of the stacks was a miner's helmet with a light.

Josh moved closer to inspect the sacks of white. If he had to guess, it was meth. Had Savannah interrupted a drug ring using the tunnels to transport their product? It would appear so.

He frowned and looked around again. Who did this garage belong to? He had a feeling of déjà vu, as if he'd seen this place before, although certainly not with the drugs on the shelves.

He headed for the door that obviously led from the garage into the main house. He held his gun steady in his hand, his heart beating a frantic rhythm.

Was anybody home? He didn't hear any movement or noise coming from the other side of the door. Once again he set his flashlight down and grabbed the door-knob, hoping that the room he was about to enter was as empty as this one.

He opened the door and winced as it gave a faint groan. The door led into a kitchen and he instantly recognized it. The plain beige walls, the white blinds at the window above the sink, and the clock on the wall shaped like a gator…it was intimately familiar.

He'd sat on one of the stools at the island and eaten pizza for a Christmas party. He'd drunk many a beer on the black leather sofa in the next room.

He was in Sheriff Trey Walker's house. Those drugs were in Trey Walker's garage. No wonder the sheriff had steered the team exploring the tunnels to the ones nearest the swamp. He'd had to protect the one that would lead them here.

Fear sliced through the shock of discovery. He'd told Trey he was leaving Savannah alone. He had to get out of here. He had to get to Savannah.

He made a call to Daniel and told him to get to Trey's house and sit on it, that there was evidence that needed to be protected. After the call, he ran the way he had come, leaving through the tunnel and racing as fast as he could to get to Savannah.

He followed his purple marks until he exploded out of the exit in Mama Baptiste's shop. He didn't speak to the startled woman as he ran by her and out the front door where his car was parked.

All he could think about was that he'd not only left Savannah alone but also given her attacker a heads-up that she would be home alone.

He would process his shock at Trey's disgusting corruption later. Right now he needed to get to Savannah's house as soon as possible.

His mind was blank other than with need to protect

the woman he loved. It didn't matter that she didn't love him back. He could live with that. What he couldn't live with was being even partially responsible for anything bad that might happen to her.

His heart dropped to his feet as he saw Trey's car parked two doors down from Savannah's house. Nobody was in the car. He was with her, Josh thought. He was with her right then, and she was nothing but the person who ruined whatever drug business Trey had been conducting through the tunnels.

You ruined everything. That was what the attacker had said to her that night at the inn. Now Josh understood what she'd ruined.

Josh squealed into her driveway and was out of the car before the engine had completely shut down. As he knocked on the front door, he noted the wiring that indicated to him she'd done as she'd told him she was going to do. She'd called Buck.

But no security system would stop her from opening the door to the sheriff. She would have no fear of letting him inside. She'd have no idea that the danger to her wore the uniform of authority.

He knocked twice, and when nobody answered, he ran around to the back of the house. The back door was open, and he peeked inside and saw a half-eaten omelet on a plate on the table.

He stepped inside, and it took him only minutes to clear the entire house. Nobody was home. He stepped out the back door and looked around. Trey's car was here. He couldn't have taken her anyplace far.

He stared at the bush and knew with a heart-stopping certainty that Trey had taken her underground to kill her.

TREY HADN'T TAKEN her far before he tied her hands behind her back. "Why are you doing this? What have I done to you?" Savannah asked in tears as they went deeper and deeper into the maze of passageways. Trey remained silent, his gun shoved hard against her back.

"Please, Trey, just let me go. I don't know anything about anything. I don't know what I've done. I don't know what you've done. If you'll just let me go, I'll forget all about this. I swear I won't tell anyone."

"Shut up." Trey finally spoke, his voice harsh. "I don't want to hear your sniveling another minute."

They continued to walk the earthen burrow, and as they did, thoughts flew through Savannah's head. She knew she was never going to leave these tunnels alive. She didn't understand why, but she'd been marked for death, and these were her final minutes on earth.

For the first time in two years, she realized she didn't want to die. She wanted to live, and not just the way she'd been living. Josh had been right. She'd been going through her life like Shelly's ghost, but she wasn't a ghost, and Shelly would have wanted far better for her.

She'd been foolish to believe that she could go through the rest of her life only holding on to memories and not realizing she needed to love and be loved, to build new memories and live life to the fullest.

Shelly would have wanted that for her, and instead

of the silly ghost walks to pay tribute to her sister, her tribute should have been to live well and find happiness. Like Josh had done…he'd lived his life as a tribute to his brother.

Now it was too late. Trey had taken her down so many tunnels she was utterly lost, her sense of direction had abandoned her and if he shot her now she suspected nobody would hear the blast of his gun.

"Was it you who attacked me at the inn?" she finally asked, needing some answers before the horrible end she knew awaited her.

Trey didn't reply.

"At least tell me what I've done before you kill me," she exclaimed. She stopped walking and turned to face him, his flashlight a blinding beam in her eye. "Don't I have a right to know?"

"Your stupid walks pretending to be your sister's ghost got in the way of a lucrative business."

"What kind of business?"

"I guess it doesn't matter what you know now. Occasionally a fishing boat comes into the lagoon carrying packets of crystal meth. This often happens on a Thursday or Friday night…the same nights you were in the tunnels. We unloaded the packets and carried them through the tunnel to a holding area, where eventually it was distributed to a handful of drug runners."

She stared at him in shock. Drug trafficking? "Who else is involved in this besides you?" She was stunned at his words, at his utter lawlessness, but she wanted all the answers before she died.

"Enough talk. Keep walking," he snarled.

They didn't walk too much farther before they reached a deep alcove set back in the tunnel wall. "Inside, against the back," he instructed her.

She wanted to balk, especially when she saw wires that indicated the entrance of the alcove was rigged with explosives. So, he didn't intend to shoot her. He was going to blast the explosives and bury her alive.

She turned and tried to rush him, hoping to push him aside and run, but he easily shoved her backward, his gun leveled at her center. "Doesn't matter to me how this gets done," he said. "I can either shoot you or blow you up. Now get to the back like I told you."

A bullet would end things immediately. As Savannah walked to the back of alcove, she realized she still entertained a modicum of hope that she'd be saved.

"Sit down with your legs out in front of you," Trey commanded.

She did as he asked, and while he tied her ankles together with rope, any thought of escaping on foot disappeared. She'd thrown Josh out of her house and had said some terrible things to him. This was all her fault. If she hadn't been so afraid to embrace Josh's love, he would still have been at the house when Trey had shown up at the back door.

The only hope she had now was that Josh would have cooled down enough to return to pack his clothes. He'd realize she was gone and go hunting for her. She didn't know if he'd figure out she was down in the tunnels or not.

All she could do now was pray that he'd somehow find her before Trey set off the explosives that would bury her forever.

"How could you be a part of this, Trey? As a law enforcement official, was the money good enough to twist you?" she asked.

"Better than good enough," he replied and leaned against the wall as if he had all the time in the world. "I now own part interest in the amusement park that's going to make me a very wealthy man. I sure as hell wouldn't have been able to do that on my sheriff's salary."

"So this was all about money." As long as she kept him talking, she gave Josh more time to find her. "Was it worth it to sell your soul?"

He laughed. "What makes you think I had a soul to start with?"

"Did you kill my sister? Did she somehow find out something that put your operation at risk?"

"No way," he replied. "I still believe Bo McBride killed your sister, but I had nothing to do with her death. The deal with the amusement park wasn't even a thought then."

With each moment that ticked by, Savannah's hope of rescue diminished. "What are you waiting for?" she finally asked. Just sitting here, waiting for death, filled with regrets, felt like a particular form of torture.

"The boss to arrive," he replied.

"Who is the boss?"

"It doesn't matter to you. You'll be dead in a matter of minutes."

A dark figure appeared behind Trey. Savannah assumed it was the boss, come to witness or make sure that the explosives rigged were appropriately set.

"Put the gun down, Trey." Trey stiffened, and Savannah rejoiced as she heard the deep, familiar sound of Josh's voice. He'd found her. She didn't know how, and at the moment she didn't care. All she knew was that she was saved.

"You wouldn't shoot a man in the back, would you, Josh?" Trey asked.

"Try me," Josh replied in a harsh voice. "Besides, you aren't a man. You're vermin preying on the town and on the woman I love. Try me, Trey. I'm more than itching to put a bullet in your back."

Trey slowly lowered his gun and set it on the ground. Josh turned on a flashlight and shone it on Savannah. "You okay?"

"I am now," she replied with a sob of relief.

Before they could exchange another word, Josh was hit in the back of the head and fell to the ground, his flashlight falling from his hand. Mayor Jim Burns stepped over Josh's body and looked at Trey in disgust.

"Good thing I came along when I did," he said.

"I just want to get this done," Trey replied and picked up his gun from the ground. "I never had the stomach for this kind of thing, and now we have two to kill instead of one."

Savannah was in a state of shock. Jim Burns was the

boss man? Josh had found her, but now he was going to die along with her. She wished he'd never found her.

"You knew the risks," Jim replied. "This has to be done to protect our investments."

Jim moved to what appeared to be a timing device connected to the wires. "I'll give us ninety seconds to get far enough away before the blast."

"How about two minutes?" Trey replied. "Just in case we've miscalculated the distance to safety or we stumble on the way out."

Savannah watched in horror as Jim nodded and set the timer. The two men went running out of the alcove and down the tunnel to the left.

She looked at the unconscious Josh.

They had two minutes to live.

Chapter Fourteen

The minute the two men ran, Josh jumped to his feet. The blow to his head hadn't knocked him out, but he'd played possum, knowing he stood no chance against two armed men.

Savannah gasped as he grabbed his flashlight and then raced to her and scooped her up in his arms. He ran down the tunnel to the right, unsure where he was going but knowing he needed to get as much distance as possible between themselves and the alcove that was about to explode.

He had no idea how much explosive they might have set, but if it was enough it might take down not just the alcove but the entire tunnel system. The explosion would shoot out and the force would follow the tunnels, potentially bringing with it fire and total destruction.

Josh tried to hold Savannah while at the same time wielding a flashlight so he didn't run face first into a wall. His heart pounded with the tick-tock of a countdown to detonation.

Savannah didn't say a word, nor did he attempt any

conversation. All he cared about was getting away from the alcove, as far and as fast as possible.

The deep rumble of the explosion erupted from someplace behind them, but instantly he felt the force of displaced air at his back. He immediately set Savannah on the ground and shielded her with his body, unsure what else to expect.

The earth shook around them, and dirt and rock fell from the ceiling, pummeling Josh on his back. Dust filled the air, choking them both. Then silence.

He remained on top of her, trying to catch his breath and waiting to make sure no more earth would shift. He finally sat up. He first looked down at Savannah, who appeared to be all right, and then shone his light ahead and through the dust-filled air. He was grateful to see that the tunnel hadn't caved in.

"We've got to get out of here," he said, unsure how solid the tunnel structure really was now. Once again he scooped her up in his arms and continued forward, seeking any exit that would take them up and out.

It felt as if he walked forever before he realized that somehow they had wound around and were now in the main tunnel that ran between Savannah's house and the swamp.

He carried her up and out by the bush in her backyard and hurried into her back door. He set her on the edge of a kitchen chair and then rummaged in the drawer for a knife to cut the ropes that tied her wrists and ankles.

She was covered in dust, including her face, making

her brown eyes appear even larger than usual. When he freed her, she jumped up off the chair and wrapped her arms around his neck.

He held her tight, thanking every deity he could think of that he'd found her in time, that she was safe and sound. While he would have liked to stand and hold her forever, he was aware that this wasn't done yet.

He released her and stepped back. "I've got bad guys to get in jail. You lock yourself in here and stay hidden so nobody knows you're home. Don't show your face until you hear me calling to you."

"Do you think anyone heard the blast?" she asked.

"Doubtful, but I'll know when I talk to Daniel. If anyone heard it somebody would have reported it by now."

He pulled his cell phone out of his pocket. Right now he had an advantage since Jim Burns and Trey Walker believed he was dead. As long as they continued to believe that, he had some time to get things into place for a takedown of the two top authority figures of the town.

He called Daniel, and for the next fifteen minutes the two men set into place what needed to be done. "Come by Savannah's when you have things in place," he said and then hung up.

"I'm going to change clothes," he said to Savannah. "You make sure the alarm is set and then stay away from any windows, and Daniel told me there's been no report of an explosion."

He first went into the bathroom and used a washcloth to clean away any dirt that was present on his face, neck and chest. He left the bathroom and entered the spare room, where he quickly changed into a clean pair of jeans and a button-down white dress shirt.

When he left the bedroom, he found Savannah sitting on the edge of the tub in the bathroom, still covered with dirt. "Are you going to be okay here alone?" he asked.

She nodded. "As long as the bad guys believe I'm dead. Jim Burns and Trey Walker are influential people. Are you going to be able to have them charged and arrested?"

"Trey has a garage full of evidence, and I have a feeling once he's under arrest he'll turn on Jim like a gator twirling to catch a fish."

"You'll come back here when it's all over?" She looked achingly vulnerable, and he wanted nothing more than to take her in his arms once again.

But he had no right. She'd made it clear to him where they stood with each other before he'd left her house earlier. When he'd taken care of Jim Burns and Trey Walker and the danger was gone, he'd return here to pack his bags and leave her life forever. "I'll be back," he replied.

She stood. "I'm going to take a long, hot bath."

"If I'm gone when you get out, you'll know Daniel picked me up."

She gave him the alarm code to leave the house and rearm the system when he did.

He left the bathroom and closed the door behind

him. She'd be fine without him now. She would choose whatever life she wanted without him in it.

He went into the living room and stood next to the window, where he could peer out but couldn't be seen by anyone. He was still shocked to learn that his boss and the mayor of the town had been in cahoots in a drug trafficking ring. Who else might be involved?

He was eternally grateful that when he'd gone down into the tunnels in search of Savannah, he'd managed to follow the sound of Trey's voice to find and save her. And his heart ached with the knowledge that his time with her had come to an end.

He would never again see her smile at him across the breakfast table. He would never hear her laugh again as he regaled her with one of his stories from his youth.

He'd never know what might have been if she'd loved him.

He hadn't loved Savannah just for the past two weeks. He felt as if he'd loved her for his whole life. He shook his head as if the motion could dislodge the pang in his heart.

Daniel had been equally shocked when Josh had shared with him what had happened and what he had learned. Hopefully he had managed to do what Josh had asked, and by the time darkness fell, the town would be rid of two nefarious characters who had abused their positions of power.

Daniel pulled up, and Josh quickly punched the numbers in to allow him to leave without setting off the alarm. He made sure it was secure again and then raced to jump into the passenger seat of Daniel's car. Daniel roared away from the curb.

"Did you get what I wanted?" he asked his friend and coworker.

"You're lucky I'm good friends with Judge Bolton. He was a bit reluctant to issue a search warrant, but he was more ticked off by the idea of a corrupt cop and mayor, so he signed off on it."

"They aren't just corrupt. They tried to kill Savannah and me," Josh said tersely. "My greatest pleasure will be getting handcuffs on both of them."

Daniel cast Josh a grin. "I knew you didn't have your cuffs with you, so I brought a spare pair. I also know that Trey left the station about twenty minutes ago, so he should be home by now, enjoying a cold beer and dreaming of his future wealth."

"That's just the way I want him, feeling safe and secure until I show up and destroy his world." Josh thought of the vision of Savannah huddled at the back of the alcove, waiting for death to come to her, and his anger at the two men responsible grew.

"Let's just hope he isn't moving the product you saw in his garage as we speak," Daniel said.

"I doubt it. With him believing that Savannah and I are dead, he has no reason to be in a hurry." Josh sat forward in his seat as they turned onto the block where Trey's home was located.

The only car parked in front of the sheriff's house was his patrol car. A light shone from the living room window, and all looked peaceful and normal.

"I want to be the first person he sees when he opens his door," Josh said. "You back me up."

"Got it."

They pulled into the driveway and walked to the front door. Josh knocked, and when his boss answered, Trey's eyes opened wide and then narrowed. "You can't prove anything," he said immediately. "It's your word against mine. I'm the sheriff of this town, and you're just a disgruntled employee I've been having problems with lately."

Daniel cleared his voice and stepped into view. He held out a piece of paper. "We're here to serve a search warrant for these premises."

"And we're going to start our search in your garage," Josh added.

Trey tried to push past the two men, but Josh grabbed him by the arm, twirled him around and snapped handcuffs on his wrists.

"Now let's take a look in your garage." Josh grabbed Trey's elbow and led him to the evidence that would be the end of life as Trey knew it.

It WAS AFTER TEN when Daniel finally dropped Josh back at Savannah's house. The place was dark and looked as if nobody was home. Apparently Savannah had taken his advice to heart and hadn't turned on lights to indicate that anyone was there.

"Savannah," he yelled through the door.

She immediately opened the door and let him inside. "Is it done?"

He nodded and turned on the end table lamp in the living room. "It's over. Trey and Jim are both behind bars and will face a judge sometime tomorrow. We also arrested Ray McClure on suspicion of conspiracy."

She sat on the sofa and motioned for him to join her. Dressed only in a short gold-colored nightgown and matching robe, with her hair shiny and her brown eyes sparkling with gold flecks, she broke his heart all over again.

"We don't know for sure what Ray's involvement might be. He swears he knew nothing about the drugs, but he was Trey's right-hand man, so the jury is out on whether he was part of the crime," he continued.

"Trey started singing like a bird once we had him in custody. Apparently both he and Jim were investing heavily in the amusement park, and he told us it was Jim who attacked you at the inn. Jim wanted revenge on you because you brought attention to the tunnels."

"Did he say who grabbed me in the tunnels?" she asked.

"Apparently that was Trey. He wanted to scare you enough that you'd stay out of the tunnels forever. Apparently he didn't intend to hurt you."

"I wish he'd told me that. So, what happens now at the sheriff's office? With the mayor? Who is going to be in charge?" she asked.

"Daniel will probably step in since he's the chief deputy sheriff, but to be honest, I'm not sure what's going to happen. It's possible that because nobody knows the depth of corruption, the department of justice or attorney general will have to come in to sort things out."

He forced a smile at her. "So, it's done. You're finally safe now, and I'll just get my things and let you have your life back."

He started to stand, but she grabbed him by the forearm and pulled him back down on the sofa. "It's not over yet." Her eyes simmered with an emotion he couldn't read, but a small fist of anxiety curled in the pit of his stomach.

She tucked a strand of hair behind her ear and stared at a point just above his shoulder, nervous tension rocketing through her. "I said some terrible things to get you out of the house. I didn't mean them. I know you weren't responsible for the investigation into Shelly's death. I wanted you out because you scared me, Josh." She looked at him. "Everything about you scared me."

"Why?" he asked in obvious confusion.

"Because you are vibrant with energy and a love of life. Because you forced me out and back into the world I thought had betrayed me by taking Shelly away."

"As I recall, I said some pretty rough things as I made my exit from here," he replied.

She smiled ruefully. "You spoke the truth. I had become a ghost. I'd given up on life and on any idea of finding happiness. It just felt like a betrayal of Shelly."

"I remember the first time I went out with friends after Jacob died. A bunch of our friends were going to a horror movie, and I decided to go after weeks of just hanging around in the house. I felt guilty the minute I got into the car. I shouldn't have been doing anything without Jacob. Then the movie started, and it was the kind of gory horror movie that Jacob loved. At that moment I felt his presence inside me, and I knew he was glad I was going on with my life."

He gazed at Savannah, knowing that his love for her shone from his eyes. "She will always be alive," he said softly. "Just like Jacob will always be alive to me. He lives on in my memories and in my heart."

"When Trey took me down in the tunnel and I knew I was probably going to die down there, I suddenly realized how much I wanted to live, how disappointed Shelly would be in me because of the choices I've made since her death. Shelly loved life. She embraced it like a favorite teddy bear, and that is what she would want me to do."

Savannah could tell by Josh's expression that he wasn't sure where this conversation was going, but she did, and she only hoped she wasn't too late.

"I shed my ghost while facing death," she continued. "I found the real Savannah again, the woman who wants to open a restaurant and laugh at silly stories. I'm the woman who loves to sit on the patio in front of the ice cream parlor and eat a waffle cone."

She moved closer to him on the sofa and saw by the look in his eyes that it wasn't too late for her, for them. "Josh, I'm the woman who was crazy about you two years ago, and now I'm the woman who is crazy in love with you."

He remained unmoving, his blue eyes shimmering. "Say it again," he demanded.

"I love you, Jo…" She didn't get the whole sentence out of her mouth before his lips claimed hers in a fiery kiss that stirred her from head to toe.

When the kiss finally ended he laughed, the sound one of pure joy. "I got the bad guys in jail and I got the girl. Life doesn't get any better than this."

"Yes, it does," she replied and snuggled against his side. "There's building a restaurant and being together and making babies."

His arm tightened around her. "I like the sound of that, especially the last part."

She smiled up at him. "The restaurant is going to take some time. But we're together now, so we could start working on the last part."

She laughed as he jumped up off the sofa and held his hand out to her. She grabbed his hand, and as he led her down the hallway toward her bedroom, she knew he was really leading her into her future…a future of happiness and laughter and love.

Epilogue

It was the beginning of a new month, and for Savannah it was the beginning of her new life. August had arrived and with it big changes not only for the town of Lost Lagoon but also for Savannah.

Although it had only been a week since she and Josh had professed their love for each other, Savannah was moving into Josh's house. Mac was thrilled that she was selling out, rubbing his hands together at the prospect of the money from the sale of the house.

Jeffrey Allen had already contacted the Realtor she'd hired to handle the sale, and negotiations were in the works even though she had yet to put a For Sale sign in the yard.

Both Trey Walker and Jim Burns were in jail, facing a variety of charges. Both men had been denied bail by the judge they had faced, despite the arguments by their lawyers.

For now Daniel was working as acting sheriff, but rumor had it that the attorney general was sending somebody in to take over and clean up any lingering corruption.

At the moment, the last thing on Savannah's mind was evildoers and town business. As she filled a box with her clothing, all she could think about was Josh and the happiness that filled her heart.

Over the past week, her love for him had only grown stronger. Once she'd truly let down her defenses, she'd allowed his love to flow over her, into her, and she'd never known that kind of joy before.

Some people might accuse her and Josh of rushing things by her selling the house and moving in with him, but she'd never been so sure of anything in her entire life.

She checked her watch. After two. She needed to leave here by three so she could get to Josh's house and have dinner waiting for him when he got home just after five.

He was on day shift now, but Savannah had already warned him not to get used to her cooking dinner for him every night. Just as she'd embraced loving Josh, she'd re-embraced her old dream of opening a fine-dining restaurant in town.

She was going to have it all, a love to last a lifetime, a successful business and eventually a family. She walked over to the desk and picked up the ceramic frog that had belonged to Shelly.

She cradled it in her hands. She would always feel grief and loss when she thought of Shelly, but with Josh's help, she'd finally moved into acceptance.

Just like Josh had told her, Shelly would always be with her, in her memories and in her heart. Even now, as the ceramic frog warmed in her hands, she felt Shelly smiling down from heaven at her.

Shelly would sing with the angels at Savannah's wedding. She'd shine down with her smile when Savannah opened her restaurant, and she'd be with her in spirit when she gave birth to her first child.

Savannah hoped someday the murder of her sister would be solved and the guilty put behind bars. But even if that never happened, she was determined to get on with her own life.

Savannah jumped as she heard the sound of the front door opening. She set the frog down in the box of clothing she had packed and hurried down the hall to see Josh.

"Hey, what are you doing here?" she asked.

As he walked toward her, his lips formed that sexy smile that she knew would warm her heart for the rest of her life. "I was in the neighborhood and decided I needed a kiss." He pulled her into his arms.

She smiled up at him. "Do you always just stop in at some random house when you're on duty and feel the need for a kiss?"

"Nah, I'm very picky. I only stop to get a kiss from the woman I'm going to marry."

"Good answer, Deputy Griffin," she said just before his mouth slanted to hers in a kiss that told her everything she needed to know about her future…and it was going to be magnificent.

* * * * *

I N T R I G U E

Available November 17, 2015

#1605 TAKING AIM AT THE SHERIFF
Appaloosa Pass Ranch • by Delores Fossen
Sheriff Jericho Crockett is stunned when his ex-flame Laurel Tate announces
that he's her baby's father and begs him to marry her to protect their child from
a killer. Can Jericho solve a murder in time to save his newfound family?

#1606 KANSAS CITY CONFESSIONS
The Precinct: Cold Case • by Julie Miller
Katie Rinaldi's son wants a dad for Christmas—and KCPD detective Trent Dixon
is at the top of his list. But a criminal mastermind may destroy all of them before
Katie and Trent can put their pasts behind them and come together as a family...

#1607 MISSING IN THE GLADES
Marshland Justice • by Lena Diaz
When former detective Jake Young's first case as a PI brings him to the town of
Mystic Glades in search of a missing person, he'll wind up fighting to survive and
to save a mysterious young woman running from her past.

#1608 AGENT BRIDE
Return to Ravesville • by Beverly Long
Former Navy SEAL Cal Hollister has vowed to protect the amnesiac bride he
calls Stormy, but can he solve the mystery of her past before the terrorists
chasing her can enact their plot to kill thousands?

#1609 SHADOW WOLF
Apache Protectors • by Jenna Kernan
Witnessing a cartel killing has put aid worker Lea Atlaha in the hands of Apache
border patrol agent Kino Cosin. To put away his father's murderer, Kino will need
to keep her alive—which will mean staying very close to her.

#1610 COWBOY UNDERCOVER
The Brothers of Hastings Ridge Ranch • by Alice Sharpe
When Lily Kirk's son is abducted, rancher Chance Hastings goes undercover
to return him home safe. But once the boy is back in his mother's arms, can
Chance convince Lily they belong on his ranch—forever?

REQUEST YOUR FREE BOOKS!
2 FREE NOVELS PLUS 2 FREE GIFTS!

H⊕**HARLEQUIN®**

INTRIGUE

BREATHTAKING ROMANTIC SUSPENSE

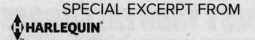
"I won't let him hurt you, Sunshine. I won't let him hurt
Tyler, either."

She nodded at the promise murmured against the
crown of her hair. But the tears spilling over couldn't
quite believe they were truly safe, and Katie snuggled
closer. Trent slipped his fingers beneath her ponytail and
loosened it to massage her nape. "What happened to that
spunky fighter who got her baby away from Craig Fairfax
and helped bring down an illegal adoption ring?"

Her laugh was more of a hiccup of tears. "That girl
was a naive fool who put a lot of lives in danger. I nearly
got Aunt Maddie killed."

"Hey." Trent's big hands gently cupped her head and
turned her face up to his. His eyes had darkened again.
"That girl is all grown up now. Okay? She's even smarter
and is still scrappy enough to handle anything."

Oh, how she wanted to believe the faith he had in her.
But she'd lost too much already. She'd seen too much.

She curled her fingers into the front of his shirt, then smoothed away the wrinkles she'd put there. "I'm old enough to know that I'm supposed to be afraid, that I can't just blindly tilt at windmills and try to make everything right for everyone I care about. Not with Tyler's life in my hands. I can't let him suffer any kind of retribution for something I've done."

"He won't."

Her fingers curled into soft cotton again. "I don't think I have that same kind of fight in me anymore."

"But you don't have to fight alone."

"Fight who? I don't know who's behind those threats. I don't even know what ticked him off. It's just like my dad all over again."

"Stop arguing with me and let me help."

"Trent—"

His fingers tightened against her scalp, pulling her onto her toes as he dipped his head and silenced her protest with a kiss. For a moment, there was only shock at the sensation of warm, firm lips closing over hers. When Trent's mouth apologized for the effective end to her moment of panic, she pressed her lips softly to his, appreciating his tender response to her fears. When his tongue rasped along the seam of her lips, a different sort of need tempted her to answer his request. When she parted her lips and welcomed the sweep of his tongue inside to stroke the softer skin there, something inside her awoke.

Don't miss
KANSAS CITY CONFESSIONS
by USA TODAY *bestselling author Julie Miller,*
available in December 2015 wherever
Harlequin Intrigue® books and ebooks are sold.

www.Harlequin.com

Turn your love of reading into
rewards you'll love with

Harlequin My Rewards

**Join for FREE today at
www.HarlequinMyRewards.com**

Earn **FREE BOOKS** of your choice.

Experience **EXCLUSIVE OFFERS** and contests.

Enjoy **BOOK RECOMMENDATIONS**
selected just for you.

PLUS! Sign up now
and get **500** points
right away!

Earn
FREE
REWARDS
Join
Today!
HarlequinMyRewards.com

MYR16R

Love the Harlequin book you just read?

Your opinion matters.

Review this book on your favorite
book site, review site, blog or your own
social media properties and share
your opinion with other readers!

THE WORLD IS BETTER WITH

Romance

2171

Harlequin has everything from contemporary, passionate and heartwarming to suspenseful and inspirational stories.

Whatever your mood, we have a romance just for you!

Connect with us to find your next great read, special offers and more.